THE ASSASSINATION OF GOVERNOR BOGGS

THE ASSASSINATION OF GOVERNOR BOGGS

ROD MILLER

BONNEVILLE BOOKS
SPRINGVILLE, UTAH

ISBN 13: 978-1-59955-863-9

Published by Bonneville Books, an imprint of Cedar Fort, Inc., 2373 W. 700 S., Springville, UT 84663
Distributed by Cedar Fort, Inc., www.cedarfort.com

LIBRARY OF CONGRESS CATALOGING-IN-PUBLICATION DATA

Miller, Rod, 1952- author.
  The assassination of Governor Boggs / Rod Miller.
    pages cm
  Summary: A fictionalized reinvestigation of the attempted murder of Governor
Lilburn Boggs in 1842.
  ISBN 978-1-59955-863-9
  1. Boggs, Lilburn W., 1792-1860--Fiction. 2. Missouri--History--Fiction.
3. Church of Jesus Christ of Latter-day Saints--History--Fiction. 4.
Mormon Church--Fiction. I. Title.
  PS3613.I55264A94 2011
  813'.6--dc22

                              2011003904

Cover design by Danie Romrell
Cover design © 2011 by Lyle Mortimer
Edited and typeset by Kelley Konzak

Printed in the United States of America

10 9 8 7 6 5 4 3 2 1

Printed on acid-free paper

Dedicated to my families:

Renee, Zeb, Pam, and Denise

and

Susan, Kate, Lisa, Sydney, and Ian

Other Books by Rod Miller

Gallows for a Gunman
Massacre at Bear River: First, Worst, Forgotten
American Heroes: John Muir, Magnificent Tramp
Things a Cowboy Sees and Other Poems
Newe Dreams: Poems by Rod Miller

QUINCY WHIG
Quincy, Illinois, Sat. May 21, 1842

ASSASSINATION OF EX-GOVERNOR BOGGS OF MISSOURI.

Lilburn W. Boggs, late Governor of Missouri, was assassinated at his residence in Independence, Missouri, by an unknown hand, on the 6th inst.

CASE NOTES OF CALVIN POGUE

When, finally, I interrogated Porter Rockwell at the tag end of this case, I asked him about Missouri and about Boggs. He poured us each the first of many "squar"—or "neat," as most would say—whiskeys, carefully raised his glass with an exclamation of "Wheat!," drained the drink, and then poured another.

I found him in the public room at the Salt Lake House. I faced Rockwell in an overstuffed chair as he sat in a ladder-backed chair, leaned back, and precariously propped against the wall. On a small table beside him sat a bucket of beer along with a mug, a tumbler, and a bottle of whiskey. Between bouts with the bucket and bottle, the notorious gunman occupied his time with the only other object on the table—a block of soft wood, pine I surmised, at which he carved and whittled with a jackknife, littering his lap and the carpeted floor at his feet with shavings.

He was an imposing figure, even at his age—which was, according to my calculations, somewhere in the middle of his fifties. His beard was long and as much gray as brown. His hair, the same. This day it flowed loose around his neck and shoulders, hanging a good half a foot if not more down his back and chest. His eyes were sharp and blue (if slightly bloodshot) and pierced like cold lightning. He was barrel-chested and thick, but you wouldn't call him fat. The hands doing the whittling were so small and thin they seemed out of place on his heavy arms.

As distinctive as the rest of the man was his voice—high in register and given to breaking, and shrill, even squeaky, when excited. And he got excited more than once in the course of our interview.

I have set down here for the case file exactly what he said, as nearly accurate as I can make it, from notes taken during our long conversation.

You want to know if I shot Lilburn Boggs, eh?
Well, if I did, you've got to prove it. They couldn't hang it on me back then and you won't do it now.

Sure, I was in Missouri at the time. Close to Independence, even. Never said I wasn't. I was in Missouri lots of times. Spent more time in Missouri than any a man ought to and no man in his right mind would do. If ever I doubted anything Joseph said—which I never did—it was that Missouri is God's own promised land. Oh, I suppose the land itself would do, but them Missouri pukes was the worst excuse for God's children ever created. More like the devil's kin if you're askin' me.

Independence, now that wasn't much more than a hog wallow. Merchants there gouged Santa Fe traders for a living. Before that, they bilked Indians and fur trappers. Wasn't a one of them anywheres thereabouts knew thing one about turnin' an honest dollar. Bunch of layabouts, is all. Them as wasn't in the mercantile business scratched around in the dirt and called themselves farmers, but they wasn't inclined to break much ground any more'n they was inclined to break a sweat. Mostly sat about on whatever porch was handy, scratchin' and spittin' and sippin' corn liquor. Squabblin' and fightin' was their favorite pastime if ever they mustered up the energy for it.

Them pukes had no use for us Mormons from the minute we showed up there around Independence back in '31. Just associatin' with Mormons—never mind bein' one—was cause enough for them pukes to pester you at any encounter. We was harassed and abused more or less every minute we was there.

I wasn't much more than a button when first I got to Missouri, along about eighteen in my years. We came from Kirtland, Ohio, aboard flatboats when Joseph sent us out there as part of the first bunch of Mormons to settle in Zion.

Pa built a ferry at the Big Blue River ten or so miles west of Independence, and I went partners helpin' run the thing. Courted Luana when I could get to town. Wed her in the winter of '32. First Mormons ever to be married in Jackson County, we was. Built us a log house next to Pa's at the ferry landin' and took up married life.

Ferryin' weren't much of a livin', but it kept us fed and sheltered. And we got along fine enough until real trouble kicked up between us and them Missouri mobocrats. Why, them pukes even tried to *haul us into court in '33 for runnin' that ferry without havin' no license. Which was, of course, nonsense. There weren't no such thing as a license, and they did it just so's to irritate us, us bein' Mormons and all.*

And them bein' pukes.

ONE

LILBURN BOGGS WAS NEVER the same after getting shot in the head.

Or so Calvin Pogue heard from Bill Boggs.

The fact that the man was anything at all after getting shot was something of a wonder, given the nature of his wounds. Four of Independence, Missouri's finest physicians treated the ex-governor's injuries and agreed he would not last the night. News of the assassination spread quickly, reported in newspapers far and wide.

But the news was premature, as he lasted the night and nearly eighteen years more.

The assassination of Governor Boggs went wrong in the dark and the rain of the evening of May 6, 1842. As Bill would tell Pogue, the family had eaten supper that evening as always, and, as always, his father retired to the sitting room with the newspaper.

Less than four feet away, storm-spattered window glass exploded in a powder blast and shower of buckshot.

Seventeen double-ought balls sprayed the room. Most blew past Boggs—barely missing Bill's six-year-old sister, he said, as she rocked a baby sister's cradle—leaving thirteen pockmarks trickling plaster dust down the wall beyond.

Four balls found their mark. Two ripped into the left side of Boggs's head and tore through the skull and into the brain. One shredded the muscles of his neck and lodged in the gore. The fourth burned through the back of his neck and roof of his mouth and was swallowed with a gout of blood as his head flopped over the chair back.

Hearing the uproar from the dining room, Bill, a boy of sixteen at the time, rushed into deathly stillness and drifting powder smoke to find his father helplessly gushing lifeblood and his sisters in stunned silence. Leaving the rest of the family to deal with things as best they could, he ran into the town to sound the alarm.

An onlooker stumbled onto the gun later, dropped in a puddle near the shattered window. Others noted boot prints in the mud, obviously left by the lurking assassin, but they were soon trampled out by the curious crowd. The gun, a large German holster pistol, was later identified by a storekeeper as stolen from his shop.

Police investigations were unable to turn up enough evidence to convict anyone.

That no one paid for the crime rankled Bill Boggs ever after. Especially, he said, since everyone knew who did it. But his father forbad him to act on that knowledge, as he feared the guilty party, if pressed, might return to finish the job.

He feared as much every day for the rest of his life.

But with ex-Governor Boggs dead and gone—of more or less natural causes—Bill Boggs intended, these many years later, to see justice done.

And so began Calvin Pogue's involvement in the assassination of Governor Boggs, in answer to a letter:

Napa, California, 6 May 1867

Mr. Allan Pinkerton
Pinkerton National Detective Agency
Chicago

Sir:
 Having become somewhat familiar with your firm and its activities in newspaper reports from the late war and since, I wish to engage your services.

Twenty-five years ago this date in Missouri, then the place of our family's residence, my father, Lilburn W. Boggs, ex-governor of the state, was victim of a crime most heinous. Results of investigations into the affair were inconclusive and unsatisfactory. While the guilty party was arrested, a grand jury would not issue an indictment on account of the evidence against him seeming insufficient to attain a verdict at trial.

The reputation of your firm and its investigative techniques leads me to believe that, even at this late date, a thorough and professional vetting of the facts would answer the question, and, if legal recourse is no longer available, at the least satisfy the longings of our family to bring the affair to a conclusion of sorts and convict, if only in the court of public opinion, the man who has caused us innumerable hours of grief and anger.

Please, sir, send to me here one of your agents for a full accounting of the particulars of the incident and surrounding events. The family stands willing and able to engage your firm at the usual and customary fees for services rendered.

Respectfully yours &c. &c.,
s/William M. Boggs

Refolding the correspondence for perhaps the hundredth time, Pogue tucked it into the inside pocket of his suit coat; winced as he used both hands to shift his leg, seeking a more comfortable position; removed his hat; and leaned against the side of the stagecoach with the hope of a short nap before reaching Sonoma, where he expected to be met by the letter's author.

The assignment to visit Bill Boggs was his, owing mostly to happenstance and convenience. Pogue had lately concluded a case involving the United States Navy in San Diego, so it was a simple matter for the head office in Chicago to reach him there with instructions to book passage on a sailing ship up the coast to San Francisco, thence northward overland by local conveyance to the Napa Valley and Mr. Boggs.

ROD MILLER

When sent to see Bill Boggs, Pogue had been in the employ of
the agency some five years, having found a place with Mr. Pinkerton after mustering out of the Army with wounds that rendered
his left leg unsuitable for further military service. His work for
Pinkerton had kept him largely in the West—Texas, California,
Utah Territory, Colorado, Montana, and Wyoming became intimately familiar to him in the years before and after the visit to Bill
Boggs. That case alone would send him, after California, eastward
to Illinois and Missouri, then again to the West to visit Utah.

The Boggs incident proved a puzzle to Pogue. The answer was
forever there, but ever out of reach. But the agent found it intrigu-
ing and was obsessive, even. And he would keep at it until he
understood the hows and whys of the assassination of Governor
Boggs.

Or not.

TWO

BILL BOGGS MET POGUE at the Sonoma station as planned. Trunk and luggage loaded in the carriage, Boggs intended to start immediately for the family home in Napa, where sleeping quarters had been arranged.

Pogue changed his mind on both counts.

"My working habits are not conducive to family life," the Pinkerton agent told him. "I am as likely as not to be up all hours of the night examining documents and writing reports. Often I pace endlessly in thought, with frequent comings and goings to walk the streets.

"My eating habits, too, are unconventional, and no person not hired for the job should be expected to cater to them."

"Surely, Mr. Pogue, my wife and her maid can accommodate your every wish," Bill said.

"No, no. It is more trouble than I am worth, I assure you. I have been told as much on many occasions. My only and every wish at this moment is to tuck into a meal and settle into a hotel."

"But sir! It is long past dinner with supper hours away. How could you possibly eat at this hour?"

"It will be no trouble, as you shall see, Mr. Boggs. I do not travel well on a full stomach and so eat little or nothing while on the road," Pogue told him. "Just as my most productive working hours seldom conform to the norm, my eating habits do not obey the routine."

"As you wish, Mr. Pogue."

"Please, Mr. Boggs, call me Pogue. Just Pogue. Or Cal, if you'd rather. Whenever I hear 'Mr. Pogue' I instinctively look around for my father—which is a futile thing, what with him long dead."

"Well enough, Pogue." Boggs laughed. "And you, you're to call me Bill. There's never been a 'mister' in my family. I don't like it for myself, and father always preferred 'Governor.'"

He reined up the team before a likely looking eatery. Next door, just past an intervening alleyway, stood a three-story hotel of a type familiar to business travelers in most every large town and small city in the West.

"Join me for a bite, won't you, Bill? We'll get started on what happened to the governor," Pogue said.

"Oh, I can't be eating this time of day. Dinner hasn't left me and supper will be waiting. But a cup of good coffee and a slice of pie wouldn't be unwelcome," Boggs said. "The pies here, by the way, can make a man squat on his haunches and beg like a dog. You'd best plan to finish off every meal with a slice, never mind the odd hours you choose to take your nourishment."

Pogue stiff-legged his way into the hotel to arrange lodgings and instructed them to fetch his traveling trunk from Boggs's wagon and stow it in his room. By the time he reached the café, Boggs was already working on his second slice of pie. The Pinkerton man made his selections from the chalkboard and saucered his coffee before asking about the crime he was to investigate. Bill filled him in on the details of that night in Independence, Missouri.

———◆———

"Why now?" Pogue asked.

"It's as I wrote in my letter to Mr. Pinkerton. That night has haunted our family ever since. We've suffered the consequences of that gunshot these twenty-five years, and the man who shot my father hasn't. He ought to be the one who's suffered for what he done."

Pogue sipped coffee from his saucer and splashed out more to cool. "But surely you know, Bill, that it's unlikely the law can or will do anything at this late date, no matter what I'm able to learn."

"True enough. But the law ain't the only ones who can demand repayment."

"You're saying you'd forego the law and the courts and settle the matter yourself?"

Bill Boggs practically scraped the shine off the china plate, wiping at the last scraps and smears of pie with the side of his fork, and then licking and sucking the silverware clean. "Can't say what I'd do, for the truth is I don't know. But like I said, what happened that night's been bothering me long enough. Maybe just knowing for sure will put it to rest." He eyed the fork carefully, making sure he hadn't missed a smudge of fruit filling or flake of crust. "Could be I'd have him killed. Maybe kill him myself. I honestly don't know."

The ring of a china platter hitting the table punctuated Bill's statement like the period at the end of a sentence. The Pinkerton agent eyed the plate's contents with suspicion. The ham steak looked edible, if overcooked and curled at the edges. Glistening grease was already congealing on the fried potatoes and onions. He prodded the carrots for signs of life, decided they'd been suitably smothered to death in whatever sticky brown sauce clung to them, and tried a forkful. Butter and raw sugar, he thought. A little scorched, but they had probably been right tasty, if a little strong, when the cook had stirred them up for dinner.

The waitress asked, "Everythin' to your likin'?"

Pogue swallowed the too-soft, too-sweet carrots and replied in the affirmative. *Not exactly to my liking*, he thought, but about what he'd learned to expect of a mid-afternoon meal in your average eating house.

"So, are you going to tell me what it is you want me to prove?" Pogue asked around a sip of now-cool coffee from his cup.

"What do you mean?"

"Well, from the sound of your letter and something in your

voice, you seem to know who it was tried to kill the governor."

Bill tap-tap-tapped the tines of his fork on his empty pie plate for a time. He said, finally, "Yes, I got a pretty good idea. Most folks there at the time had the same idea. It ain't no secret. But maybe I oughtn't say anything—let you come to it yourself."

"No reason not to say what you know," Pogue said. "A case this old, it will be good to have some place to start. Save me some time. Besides, I'll change course soon enough anyway if I find something that points in another direction."

"Porter Rockwell."

"I've heard the name."

" 'Most everyone has," Bill said. "Leastways everybody that's spent any time anywhere between here and the Mississippi in the last twenty years. He's a real piece of work, that man."

"I'll want to hear all about it," Pogue said. He eased himself up slightly on his good leg, grabbed the arms of the chair, pushed back from the table, and then dropped the soiled napkin from his lap onto his empty plate. "First thing tomorrow. Say you meet me here at the hotel after your breakfast."

———◆———

The real trouble 'tween us Mormons and the old settlers thereabouts in Missouri commenced in '32. Some of our men was pelted with stones, houses and buildin's got torched, livestock rustled, that sort of thing. No one was killed, then, but some would have been save for luck.

It just kept buildin' up. Everything we ever did annoyed them pukes. Get a bunch of 'em and a jug of whiskey together and soon enough they'd take up pesterin' the Saints for recreation. Beatin's got to be right ordinary if ever they found a Mormon alone. Insultin' our womenfolk was a big laugh for them.

They'd loop their lassos around the ridge beam of a house and drag the roof right off. Then scatter folks's food and fixin's in the dirt, set fires, steal whatever they took a fancy to, and bust all else to pieces.

One summer day in '33, a dozen or so ornery-lookin' pukes

showed up at the ferry, and once we hauled them and their horses across, they lit out toward Independence as if late for a party. Turns out they was. They come back after sundown lookin' like they'd had a hard day's work—which I knew couldn't be the case, them bein' border trash and all. But they'd been up to somethin', for sure.

"We tore up Phelps's press and gave a couple of your friends a tar-and-featherin'," one of them said. "Unless you want a taste of the same, you'll chuck the Mormons. Understand?"

We headed for town to find out what they'd done. Near five hundred of them—must've been every man in Jackson County and for miles in every direction—had lit into the Mormons. Done what them pukes told us they did, and then some. Our little newspaper and printin' office was trashed and a bunch of homes burned out. They beat up a bunch of men and boys.

That's the first day I ever heard much about Lilburn Boggs. Oh, I knew of him before then, him bein' the lieutenant governor of our fine state and all. But never had I been told much about the man or his doin's. But he'd been there in Independence that day, which was where he lived and had been since before the town was even there. Important fellow thereabouts—leastways him and a majority vote of Missouri pukes seemed to think so.

But we was told he strolled around through the ruins of W. W. Phelps's printing business, stepping through the scattered type and scorched press sheets like some tinhorn army officer surveying a battlefield.

"You now know what our Jackson boys can do," he speechified to all them scared Saints tryin' to sort their lives out of the mess them mobbers left, "and you must leave the country."

What a nuisance.

THREE

AFTER THE MEAL, Pogue picked up his key from the hotel desk and made his way upstairs, swinging his stiff leg around and up to the tread on which he stood and then repeating the half-step to the top. His trunk had been shoved haphazardly through the door, left to lie in the middle of the scarce floor space between the threshold and the foot of the iron bedstead, his carpetbag perched on top.

Shoving the trunk flush against the bed, he gripped the bag and hefted it onto the mattress, unclasped it, and spread its jaws. After rummaging around for his shaving kit, he stepped to the washstand and splashed water into the basin. Pogue sloshed the tepid water onto his face with both hands and smeared his hair back with wet palms, then dragged a gap-toothed comb through, waving a hand mirror around to follow the action. Although he was not an old man, not even of middle age, he wondered at the streaks of gray scattered here and there in his otherwise dark brown mop.

He poured water from the flowered pitcher to dampen his toothbrush, dipped it into a tin of tooth powder, and gave his teeth a vigorous brushing. He held the hand mirror low and raised his chin, deciding with downcast green eyes there weren't yet enough whiskers under his Vandyke to merit a shave. Pogue next fetched a clothing brush from the carpetbag, brushed dust from the cuffs

14

of his pants, and then swiped at his jacket and the brim of his hat.

Satisfied that he was presentable, Pogue snapped the carpet-bag shut and stepped out into the hallway to brave the stairway and pay the town of Sonoma a visit.

———◆———

Two saloons and a bookshop later, Pogue opened the door of an outsized wood frame building identified by its signs as a store carrying dry goods, notions, and general merchandise.

A bell jangled as he shoved the door aside. But the clerks—a woman he could see halfway down a long aisle slapping at a high shelf with a feather duster, and an apron-clad man studying a ledger at the counter—seemed not to notice. Eyeing the goods on display as he went, Pogue wandered toward the right side of the counter.

A small keg, empty now of what likely had been a load of nails, sat on the floor at the corner of the counter, sprouting a half dozen canes and walking sticks. He hefted a few, checking their feel and balance. A cane would ease the load on his game leg, relieving some of the pain, he knew. But he thought canes were for old men, feeble men. And he was a long way from either, limp or no.

He scanned the shelves behind the counter, noting colorful exhibits of soaps, tobaccos, patent medicines, bolts of cloth, ladies' hats, trousers, shirts, collars, cravats, neckties, scarves, rebozos, ribbons, kitchen goods and gadgets, candles, candlesticks, lamps, lanterns, and on and on, row upon row, shelf upon shelf.

Only one item among the hundreds displayed caught his eye. Tucked on a shelf among China dolls, tops, tiny tea sets, and toys was a wooden horse with wheels, painted in bright blue and yellow with accents of black and white. Its tail and mane appeared to be fashioned from yellow yarn; a loop of black yarn formed the bridle rein.

"Sir?" Pogue said, to catch the attention of the clerk, whose nose was still buried in the big ledger book.

The man tucked a slip of paper between the pages to mark his place as he closed the book. He adjusted his spectacles, placed his palms on the ledger cover, looked up at Pogue, and replied. "Sir?"

"I'd like a look at that toy pony, if I may," Pogue said.

The man fetched it from the shelf and then pushed it until it rolled along the counter, wheels squeaking as the horse made its way toward the customer. The Pinkerton man watched the rolling toy approach, slow, and creak to a stop just shy of where his hand rested on the counter.

"I'll take it."

"Would you like that wrapped?"

"As a matter of fact, I would. I would like it packed and packaged and shipped to Chicago. But not today. I'll bring by a letter tomorrow to tuck in with it."

"Fair enough," the storekeeper said, then totaled up the charges and collected cash to cover Pogue's purchase with an added price for postage.

The detective jangled his way out the door and spent another hour walking the streets, then stopped at the café where he'd eaten earlier. The supper crowd had pretty much cleared out; only a few customers lingered over coffee. He ordered a thick sandwich of roast beef at the counter and asked that it be wrapped to take along. A bottle of beer while he waited tasted good, so he took two more out the door with his sandwich.

Back in his room, the detective removed his jacket and trousers and hung them neatly over the ladder back of the room's only chair.

In the carpetbag, he found a bottle of croton oil liniment, sat on the edge of the bed, and spent several minutes massaging it into his stiff knee, his fingers feeling the wrinkles and ridges of scar tissue that puckered the flesh. As he rubbed, the skin reddened with the heat, some scars turning darker, others staying smooth and white. He flexed the joint, but the action was slight. His knee would never work again, and he knew that, but it didn't hurt to try—except, that is, for the grimacing pain the trying caused.

Swinging his legs onto the bed, Pogue leaned back against

the pillow to attempt sleep. He dozed from time to time but did not think he ever drifted into a deep sleep, so he was surprised to notice the depth of darkness and the quiet when he opened his eyes. He lay still for a moment, gathering his wits and getting his bearings, then rolled out of the bed and fumbled around to light a lamp.

The letter, he remembered.

Pulling on his pants to ward off the chill, Pogue again fetched the carpetbag for his house slippers and stationery kit, then uncorked the ink bottle and a bottle of beer.

Sonoma, Calif.

My Darling Emily Elizabeth,

Here is another pony to add to your collection, or, as they say in this country, "remuda." I suppose your stable is getting quite full. I hope there is room for this one.

My work will keep me in California for a little longer, then I plan to come to Chicago for a while. I hope we can spend some time together. I bet you have grown so much I will not recognize you. Not really—I could never forget my best girl!

I hope to see you soon, Emily, and collect on all the kisses I have missed. Until then, mind your mother and your grand-parents and know that I love you.

As always,
Father

Pogue addressed an envelope, capped the ink, cleaned the nib, and set the letter aside to dry. He unwrapped his sandwich and washed it down with the second bottle of beer, wondering if his daughter would see the letter. Or the pony.

The agent put on shoes, jacket, and hat and set out to walk the streets, awaiting the arrival of morning and Bill Boggs.

It didn't get no better for us in Missouri after that day they mobbed our people. Matter of fact, it got worse. And that Lilburn Boggs was in the middle of it. Oh, he seldom, if ever, raised his own hand against a Mormon. But he never did nothin' to stop them mobbers and even egged 'em on.

It got so bad that late that next summer—would've been '34—us Mormons got up a petition to Governor Dunklin to raise some militia troops for our protection. Thing was, see, most of us was poor and you couldn't have rounded up enough arms from the whole bunch of us Mormons to put up a good fight. We was outnumbered, anyway, besides bein' outgunned. My mark was on that petition.

But with Boggs bein' lieutenant governor and livin' in the county where the trouble was, he had more influence with Dunklin than all the Saints put together. So there weren't nothin' done. Which meant them pukes could come after us whenever and wherever they took a notion to, and there weren't nothin' the government would do to help us.

So our Mormon leaders filed a lawsuit so as the courts would force the government to act. But when word of that got out, it upset them pukes all the more, and they cut loose on us again.

One evenin', 'long about the end of October, a mob forty strong rode into our little settlement there on the Big Blue River. I's out on the ferry at the time, so I didn't see the trouble nor could I do anythin' to stop it. Them pukes rode in, pulled down a dozen or so of our houses—'most every one in town—and tied up and flogged every man of us they could lay their hands on. Luana's brother George was one what got beat and whipped. And it wasn't just our town. They attacked every Mormon town along the Missouri, and for more than a week, every Saint in Missouri had reason to fear for our lives.

They came back a few days later to finish the job. Ma and Pa's roof took a tumble at the end of their ropes, and they scared my folks near to death with their threats. They even threatened to cut Ma's throat. Defenseless old woman!

They did the same to our cabin. Luana couldn't do nothin' but stand by and watch while they emptied our ruined house and broke up what furniture we had. Sliced open our feather ticks and scattered the down to the winds.

"Never again," I told myself.

If ever I had inclinations toward the Christian ways of turnin' the other cheek, they left me that day. I determined to find the means to get me some guns and learn how to use them. Them mobbin' pukes would nevermore get away with attackin' my family.

Never again.

FOUR

"PORTER ROCKWELL is as cold-blooded a man as ever drew breath," Bill Boggs told Pogue. "His murders number in the dozens, most at the behest of his superiors in that infernal church of the Mormons. He was jailed for shooting the governor, and he would be there yet had not a weakling judge turned him loose.

"But before I go any farther down that road, give me leave to tell you a bit about the governor."

The Pinkerton man shifted his chair, allowing room to stretch his bad leg beside the low table that sat between him and Boggs in the cramped hotel lobby. He retrieved his notebook and pencil from the table and nodded consent for Boggs to continue.

"Given his long service in politics, folks who did not know my father may think him a pale-faced, soft-bellied man who was most at home with his knees under a desk. No. Not the governor.

"He was a frontiersman, hard as flint and tougher than rawhide. He was in western Missouri from the first, trading with Indians and outfitting trappers at Fort Osage. He went out the Santa Fe Trail when the track was too fresh to raise dust. He married into the Bent family and had a part in their fur empire. When that woman died, he wed my mother, a granddaughter of Daniel Boone."

Pogue sat with pencil poised, enthralled with the story but not making notes from it. He failed to see how any of it would aid his investigation.

"He ran the Mormons out of Missouri and saved the state for respectable folks. And when the place became too crowded for his taste, he struck out again, coming to California in 1846, in time to help wrest this land from the Mexicans. Here, too, the governor was a leader of the people, a man respected far and wide and appointed to public office as a result.

"I say all this," Boggs said, "so you'll have some idea what kind of man it was that murdering Mormon filled with lead."

"You seem convinced it was this man Rockwell who shot your father."

"Me and hundreds of others. Pretty much everyone in Independence and for miles around at the time thought so. Except the grand jury. They might've thought so too but didn't think there was enough evidence to try him."

Pogue asked why he was so convinced and scratched rapidly across the pages of his pocket notebook as Boggs laid out his case: how Rockwell's presence around Independence came to be known, the motive for the shooting, how the gun was obtained, the Mormon's flight from the scene, the manhunt, the capture, the arrest, the release.

Boggs had prepared a list for Pogue—a lengthy roster of names of people with ties to the case, with notations of their involvement and the last-known whereabouts of some. Pogue perused the list.

"You've crossed out some of these names."

"Dead," Boggs said.

"Any of these men Rockwell's associates?"

"No. Some are Mormons, or at least used to be. Anyone loyal to that church would lie anyway—about Rockwell or any other subject their leaders told them to. John Bennett is on there—he was mayor of Nauvoo, and it was him that spilled the beans on who the assassin was and who gave the orders. But I lost track of him long ago.

"Then there's Sam Brannan. Him, I know. He was high-up among the Mormons at one time, but no more. He knew the governor. And he knows Rockwell. You'll find him in San Francisco."

Pogue said, "I told you this before, but it bears repeating. All this happened long ago. Long ago. Memories fade. It's likely that any records that were kept have been lost or destroyed. And I will be obligated to get the Mormon side of the story if this is to be a full investigation."

"I know that. All we ask is that you do what you can."

"Suppose I determine this Rockwell did not do it?"

"So be it. At least then we'll know who did."

"Maybe," Pogue said. "Maybe not. Probably not."

FIVE

CALVIN POGUE AND BILL BOGGS sat silent in the hotel lobby, each quarrying his mind for any stone left unturned.

Finally, the Pinkerton man folded his notebook closed, and as he tucked it into an inside jacket pocket, he felt the letter to Emily Elizabeth.

"I suppose I have enough to go on. At least for a start," he said.

Boggs asked, "Will I be hearing from you?"

"I'll write from time to time. Either to fill you in on what I'm learning or with questions. I cannot say when or how often. This is likely to be a drawn-out case. I believe I shall go back to San Francisco and look up this Brannan, then back to Chicago. A trip to Independence will follow. Then, who knows? I'll follow where the investigation leads.

"Just now, though, I have to deliver this letter to the store yonder way, to accompany a package home to my daughter."

"You're a family man, then?" Boggs said, surprise sitting him upright.

"I've a daughter. Why not?"

"Well, it's the traveling, I guess. From what I gather, you haven't been home for some time, and it will be some time yet before you get there."

"It would take a toll, I suspect. But any hope for my marriage was gone long before my being gone had a chance to damage it."

Boggs wondered if Pogue was uncomfortable talking about such a thing, but curiosity got the best of him. "What was it, then? The war?"

"Plenty of marriages were casualties of the war. I suppose mine was one of them, in a manner of speaking. My wife, you see, is from a prominent family in Chicago. Wealth, society, all that. Her parents didn't ever warm to me; from the start they thought me not worthy of her. Or them, for that matter.

"The thing was, they were very protective of their daughter. Too protective, I thought. That became evident when the war started and I wanted to join. They talked me out of it, then. But when the drafts started I determined to go, no matter. That led to no end of arguments. Not arguments, really. No member of that family is capable of a raised voice. So it was all very civil. My father-in-law summoned me to his office one day and all but demanded that I allow him to finance a substitute to relieve me of any responsibility. I declined. When I came home wounded, they could not resist pointing out how they had been right all along, that they had said from the start no good could come from my going off to war."

Boggs sat enthralled as Pogue related how his father-in-law offered him a place in the family business, which he did not accept, further souring the relationship. When Pogue signed on with Pinkerton's, his wife, unwilling to live away from her parents in Pogue's absence, moved with their young daughter back into her childhood home.

"Their intentions are good," Pogue said. "But I fear they are smothering the girl. They are all so afraid some calamity will befall her she is barely allowed to go alone to the privy. Emily Elizabeth's great love is horses. She's fanatical about horses. Books, pictures, you name it. But her mother and grandparents dare not let her near a live one, even going so far as forbidding her to pet the ragman's nag on the street. They could easily afford a pony for the girl. Heck, they could afford a hundred of them. But they won't do it and won't allow me to buy her one.

"So, in my travels, I am always on the lookout for toy

horses—wooden ones, ones with rockers, with wheels, cloth ones stuffed with wool, realistic or fantastic, whatever. I send them all home."

"She likes them, I'll bet," Boggs said.

"Can't say. Fact is, I can't even say she gets them. Could be her mother—or her grandparents—neglect to give her my packages or my letters. Could be they think it best not to remind the girl she has a father. Oh, they never keep me from seeing her when I'm in Chicago. But they keep our visits under a pretty tight rein. Don't want a foolhardy father allowing any damage to the girl."

Pogue sat a moment. Boggs let him.

When again the detective spoke, it was to announce his leaving.

"Anyway, there's a horse at the store for her, waiting to take this letter to Chicago. I had better get it over there."

Pogue leaned forward and used the arms of the chair to hoist himself upright, dragging his stiff leg under him as he rose. Once upright, he grasped Bill Boggs's outstretched hand.

"It is a pleasure to know you, Pogue," he said.

"Likewise, Bill Boggs. I hope we can resolve this matter to your satisfaction. I'll surely give it my best."

"I'm sure you will."

———◆———

Jackson County didn't cool off any in the days to come, and before I could get myself armed, they came again.

A few days after wreckin' our houses they showed up in numbers at the ferry. We weren't inclined to haul them mobbin' pukes across the water, so they drew down on us and took the ferry by force. A handful of 'em stayed at the landin', and the rest rode on toward Independence with blood in their eyes.

They overran some of our friends comin' to the Blue to help us, and there was some fightin'. Four Saints ended up in their graves from them skirmishes in early November. But a couple of Missouri pukes went under too.

Two of our Mormon boys was jailed for no good reason. We was gettin' better organized by then, with men from the settlements startin' to form up in groups to save ourselves. A big bunch of us—couple hundred—marched for Independence to see them prisoners freed.

Mobbers had spread the word that we had the town under siege, which weren't nowheres near true. Boggs used the confusion to get Governor Dunklin to call out the state militia to make war on us Mormons. That militia leader—can't recall his name—Pincher, Pitcher, somethin'—met us on the road with his troops. That man swore in the name and on the honor of Lilburn Boggs that them toy soldiers would protect us from the mobs, and talked our head men into us givin' up what guns we had and goin' home.

That man or Boggs or both was lyin' through their teeth as it turned out. Surrenderin' them weapons made it so much the easier for them mobbin' pukes to persecute us. They kept pushin' until they pushed us to the banks of the Missouri River and still didn't stop. 'Most every Mormon in Jackson County was forced to abandon what they had and start again with nothin' north of the river in Clay County.

'Most all of us was pretty downhearted down there on the river, waitin' for whatever might come. Them of the prayin' persuasion was at it day and night. Others of us wondered if God had forgot us altogether. Then one night in the middle of November, the stars started fallin' from the sky near thick as raindrops. They was shootin' and streakin' ever' which way, with flamin' trails long as the sky was wide. It kept up until the sunrise.

Them fallin' stars filled some of the Saints with hope, thinkin' it a sign from on high that God still had us in mind.

Me, I wasn't so sure. Nor had I any notion what them Missouri pukes made of it, either. Could be they thought it was fireworks to celebrate their victory.

SIX

San Francisco, Calif.

A. Pinkerton
Pinkerton National Detective Agency
Chicago, Ill.

Sir:

I have been to meet William M. Boggs as instructed to gain the particulars of his case. Am now in San Francisco, where I intend to look up Samuel Brannan, who has knowledge of the principals in this affair, if not the affair itself. My hope is that he will shed light on the ex-governor's character, as well as that of the man Boggs believes shot his father, one Porter Rockwell of the Mormons.

Also, as I am able, I shall look up others in this vicinity with long association with the ex-governor to learn if he talked about the murder attempt and, if so, determine if any of that information might prove helpful.

I have booked passage on a Panama ship sailing from here four days hence. As soon as connections and circumstances allow, I shall arrive in Chicago and report to you my progress and plans for further investigation of this matter.

———————◆———————

Sam Brannan was not a difficult man to locate. Practically anyone on the streets of San Francisco could say where to find him on any given day. He had been one of the city's original American settlers, having taken up residence there when the place was still known as *Yerba Buena*.

In his inquiries, Pogue learned that Brannan sailed into the bay in the summer of 1846 in a ship whose cargo consisted almost solely of Mormons. He had been something of a leader among those people, having published a newspaper for the Saints in New York and other eastern states, and had been among the sect's most influential men there.

Since stepping off the ship, he had bought and sold real estate (selling more than he ever had title to, according to some), published two newspapers, acted as a trader and merchant in San Francisco, and any number of other enterprises. He had made his fortune in the Gold Rush years, accumulating vast amounts of the precious metal by mining the miners. As owner of the only mercantile business at Sutter's Fort or anywhere else near the diggings, he extracted gold from the pockets, pokes, pans, and packs of the forty-niners without breaking a sweat.

Fact was, they said Brannan himself launched the Gold Rush, as he was the man who first sent news of the discovery to the East and walked the streets of San Francisco waving a jar of gold and shouting out news of its origin, thereby spreading a fever that affected every able-bodied man and effectively depopulated the city for a time.

Brannan's relationship with the Mormon king Brigham Young had been a rocky one. After church founder Joseph Smith's murder in Illinois, Brannan backed William Smith, a brother of the slain prophet, in his failed bid to lead the Church. Despite the unforgivable lapse in loyalty, Young—ever pragmatic—assigned

Brannan to round up the Saints in the East and arrange for their relocation in the West, out of the United States and clear of the eternal persecution of the Gentiles.

Meanwhile, Young shepherded the main flock overland from Illinois. Thousands of Mormons took the road West in search of a new home.

Brannan found one first. He beat Young to the Mexican territories of the far West by more than a year and assigned himself the task of establishing Zion in California. And he set about with his followers to do just that, pooling the resources of the people to obtain land, husband livestock and crops, establish businesses, and build a city.

"Brigham Young is a fool," Brannan told Pogue. "I rode east across the Sierra and the desert to meet him in '47, willing to act as Moses and lead God's children to the Promised Land. I found them huddled in the wasteland of the Great Salt Lake Valley, and Brother Brigham had them at work settling in at that godforsaken place. If I hadn't seen it myself, I would not have believed it.

"Why would that man think those salt flats held any promise? But he used God's name to declare it the place to build the City of the Saints. If ever any man used the Lord's name in vain, surely that was it. So I came back to Alta, California, where any fool could see there were better prospects, and eventually shed myself of the Mormons. They're still there, and I'm still here, and that suits me just fine."

Pogue asked about Porter Rockwell.

"Sure, I know Port. Haven't seen him in years and was only in his company a time or two. But that don't mean I don't know him. He's about as cold-eyed a killer as ever you'll see. They say he's murdered scores of men, and more than a few women, on Brother Brigham's orders, and I don't doubt a word of it. The last time I laid eyes on him I could see he would have killed me in an instant if only his handler gave the word."

"What was the occasion?" Pogue asked.

"A dispute over money. Back in the late forties—'49 as I recall. Maybe '50. Anyway, sometime back then. Brigham had the notion that the tithes I had collected from the Saints in California and the increase from our work here belonged in his accounts in Great Salt Lake City. Brigham, you see, is of a covetous nature where money is involved. They say the most dangerous place to be in all the West is between Brigham Young and a nickel, and I'll bear testimony to the fact.

"So he sent Amasa Lyman, one of his flunkies, over here with a demand for that money. Rockwell came along as muscle. Told them the devil would be strapping ice skates on his shoes to get to work before they saw a penny from me. Then I sent them packing."

"And they went? Packing, I mean?"

"Indeed they did. Lyman, and some of them. Oh, they didn't go immediately back to that desert they call home. Lyman stayed around another month or two. Trying to connive a way to get his hands on my money, which they never did," Brannan said.

"Rockwell, now, I came to wonder if ever he would leave. He and a partner got in the saloon business up in the mining country. Made a pretty penny too, I suspect." Brannan laughed. "What that bumpkin didn't know is that every drop of whiskey he sold he bought from me. All his hard work turned a tidy profit for me, as well."

"You did business with the man, then?"

"Oh, no. No, no. Not directly, at least. See, at the time I had my fingers in every bit of commerce in the gold fields. My store at Sutter's was the only place anyone in them hills could get supplies between there and San Francisco. So every pack train of tonsil varnish Rockwell hauled came from my warehouse. He likely had no notion that was the case and could not have done anything about it if he had. It still tickles me to think of it, though."

A knock at the door and a beckoning assistant took Brannan out of the office where Pogue had found him. "Won't be a minute," he said.

Pogue took the opportunity to stretch his legs, wincing as his weight settled on the wounded knee. He studied the furnishings and shelves for any hint they might reveal of Brannan's character, but he saw nothing. The office wasn't fancy, but neither was it shabby. The few books on the wall were the usual run of classics. A volume labeled the Book of Mormon stood among them, the leather of its spine scuffed and creased from long use. He wondered if it had been opened lately or if Brannan's disgust with the Mormons included their holy book.

He slid the book off the shelf and thumbed through it until Brannan returned.

"Ah, you're looking into my past, I see."

"Sorry, Mr. Brannan. I did not mean to intrude," Pogue said.

"No offense taken, young man. It doesn't get much use these days, I'm afraid. Now, where were we?"

"You were saying about Porter Rockwell and his saloon business."

"Ah, yes. Porter Rockwell. No one here at the time knew him by that name, of course. Went by Brown, or some such. See, he wasn't exactly a popular man them days. Nor since, as a matter of fact. Plenty of men in the diggings got here from Missouri and Illinois and Iowa, and he had a fearsome reputation around there. Not well liked, at all, was Porter Rockwell. Hundreds, maybe thousands of men would have killed him given half a chance, for reputation's sake if nothing else. So Rockwell thought it best to lie low."

"I want to ask, too, about Lilburn Boggs. I'm told you knew him."

"Oh, yes. Governor Boggs. It's likely he was one of the reasons Rockwell didn't advertise his presence here."

Pogue asked, "Was Rockwell afraid of Boggs, do you think?"

"I don't think Rockwell knows what fear is. Cautious, I'd say. Wary, maybe. But not afraid. They say his success as a killer comes from never flinching in the face of anything. They say he'll look a man in the eye as calm as you please and shoot him down while that man wonders whether to pull the trigger. Rockwell doesn't hesitate, I'm told. Just shoots. Fact is," Brannan said, "if anyone of that pair was afraid, it was Governor Boggs."

"How's that?" Pogue said. "You said no one knew of Rockwell's presence."

"Very few knew. But some did. Boggs, for one. He perked up at any mention of Mormons in the area. And he had plenty of friends around to keep him informed. Some say those same friends were out to hunt down and kill Rockwell."

"Any truth to that?"

"Oh, I don't know. It's possible, I suppose. But, more likely, the opposite was true."

"What do you mean?"

"As I said, Rockwell killed on orders from Brigham Young. As long as the man drew breath, Boggs's name was first on a long list of people the Mormons wanted dead. None of those 'Saints' would ever say so outside of their councils, but I know it to be true. That's the way they operate. Anyone crosses the Mormons, Brother Brigham sends Rockwell, or Bill Hickman, or Ephraim Hanks, or another of his hired guns to put them under.

"It's only through good luck that they didn't get me. Many's the time they tried, and, thanks be to God, they failed an equal number of times. After that disagreement over the tithing money, more than one pack of Mormon hounds came sniffing after me. I don't doubt that's why Rockwell stayed around here. It is my firm belief he had orders to do away with me and Boggs as well."

Pogue noticed the Book of Mormon still in his hands, closed it, and replaced it on the shelf. "You believe this to be true? That Rockwell was out to kill Boggs?"

"As much as I once believed that book was true."

"Can I sit, Mr. Brannan? This leg of mine doesn't fancy standing for long periods. Or sitting for long periods. But, for now, I think taking the weight off would offer some relief."

"By all means. Please, pardon my lack of manners."

Pogue lowered himself into a side chair facing the desk. Brannan went to take the other, thought better of it, and again occupied his wheeled chair opposite his guest, the desk between them. The investigator stared for a moment at his open notebook, deliberately added a few lines, and then flipped the leaf to reveal a fresh page.

"Did Rockwell take any action in that direction? You say you believe he intended to kill Boggs. Was there any overt attempt, anything in that direction you know of?"

Brannan tipped his chair back, locked his hands across his stomach, and looked to the ceiling for inspiration. "No. But then I wouldn't have known. Nor would anybody. And that would include the governor's watchdogs. You see, that's one thing everyone—friend or enemy—would agree on, come to Rockwell. He's a stealthy one. You can never tell what he's up to, even if you're sitting across from him just as you are from me. The man's as cool as meltwater. But knowing something of his history, as I do, I'd bet double eagles against acorns he didn't spend all his time here hauling whiskey or keeping bar."

"Sir?"

"Were you to ask Rockwell, and were he to answer you, I'll wager he could give you a pretty thorough rundown of the governor's habits, the layout of his house and yards, a detailed description of every horse he rode or drove, and the comings and goings of every person in the Boggs household. And it would not surprise me if, on many an occasion, Port had the man in his sights."

"Why then," Pogue asked, "did he never pull the trigger?"

"As I said, Porter Rockwell is a careful man. My guess is that he learned that the governor too was careful. Remember that Boggs had his own hard cases on the lookout. Mayhap Port decided the risk of killing Boggs was greater than the reward. Had he seen it otherwise, he'd have killed him."

After a moment or two of attention to pencil and notebook, Pogue said, "Let me back up. You said Boggs knew Rockwell was around and that fear of that knowledge led to his hiring of what you call 'hard cases.' Did the governor make—or have anyone make—any attempts on Rockwell's life?"

"Not that I ever heard tell of. That's not to say it didn't happen. There were some lonely places on those mountain roads and trails Rockwell and his pack trains traveled them days. And it would not have been in his interest to make any fuss in public about violence against himself—him needing anonymity and all."

"And you believe the governor capable of such a thing?"

"Looking over your shoulder for Mormons every hour of the

day wears on a man. That much, I know on my own. And I know that since they shot him in Missouri, Boggs feared that his life could yet be lost at the hand of Rockwell or some other of the Saints. He carried that fear across the plains with him, and they say it got worse when word came the Church also was on the trail; worse again whenever he heard of more Mormons in the area. Rockwell, especially. Such fear can drive a man to desperate measures."

"Tell me more about his coming west."

This time, it was Brannan who paused to put pen to paper. He pulled a note card off a stack on the desk, dipped a pen, and scratched out a line or two. He waved the paper gently to dry the ink and said, "I'm not the one to ask. I wasn't there and only know what I've been told. And that, not by Boggs."

He eyed the note before passing it across the desk to Pogue. "Go see this man. He knows. He can tell you."

———————◆———————

Things quieted down for the next few years in Clay County, Missouri.

Some.

There weren't many settlers thereabouts when the mobs pushed us across the river. But more and more folks moved into the area, and it seems 'most every one of them was as trashy as them pukes in Jackson County. Or they soon learned to act that way, at least so far as gettin' along—or not gettin' along—with us Mormons.

So after three years, we was made to pack up and move north yet again. Them politicians even made a new county just for the Mormons. Caldwell County. The State of Missouri set it aside for the Saints, figurin' we could live there in peace with our neighbors—on account of there wasn't any neighbors, to speak of. So more'n a thousand of us settled there.

Me and Luana had some little ones by then. Her folks had stayed down around Independence all along, figurin' the worst of it was over. But me, I wanted to get as far away from them Jackson County pukes as I could.

Along about that same time, things got rough for Joseph and the Saints still in Ohio. Seems folks around Kirtland weren't no more hospitable than them in Missouri. So another passel of Mormons showed up in Caldwell County, settlin' there and in the country thereabouts. Far West was the main settlement, but there was others scattered all around.

None of them towns amounted to much. Those of us as had been in Missouri had had all we owned stole or destroyed more'n once and so hadn't much to show. And most of them that come from Kirtland had even less. We cobbled together cabins and houses as fast as we could, but lots of folks lived in tents and wagon boxes.

It wasn't no church picnic, I can tell you that. But it would soon enough get worse.

SEVEN

JACOB WRIGHT HARLAN answered the knock and stared for a moment at the man at the door.

"Let me guess," he said after an uncomfortable silence. "You want to ask me about the Donners up at Truckee Lake."

Pogue returned the stare. Harlan looked to be something over fifty years of age, but he knew him to be nearer to forty. A long nose separated heavy, drooping lids that framed slightly bulging eyes. Skin hung slack on cheeks and jowls, suggesting weight loss. Strands of gray shot through dark hair and a Vandyke beard.

"No," Pogue said. "I don't."

"Well, I suppose you'd best come on in, then," Harlan said, pulling the door wide as he turned and walked into a dim sitting room. "I can offer you coffee left over from breakfast. But that's all. I never seem able to keep anything in the kitchen or the pantry since my wife died. I've a bottle of whiskey, if it's not too early for you."

Pogue said, "It is a mite early" and sat in a wooden chair with a woven rawhide seat that Harlan indicated with a wave of his hand. "Just conversation will be fine."

His host again studied Pogue before lowering himself into a stuffed chair. The two sat at right angles to one another, near a corner of the room occupied by a small square table cluttered with newspapers, tobacco pouch and pipe, a pair of spectacles, and an

36

assortment of stained drinking glasses and coffee mugs.

"My apologies for the state of this house. I've a cleaning woman who comes in, but tidying up's another thing I can't get the hang of since I lost my wife. It's funny the things you count on a woman for, not even realizing.

"So if you're not a curiosity seeker concerning that unfortunate trip west of which I was a part—which most every stranger who comes here is, hence my somewhat rude greeting—what brings you to my door?"

Pogue grasped his knee and slid the stiff leg to a more comfortable position before reaching inside his jacket pocket for his notebook and pencil. He turned through page after page, filled margin to margin with scribbled notes, before revealing a clean sheet.

"What I've come for does involve your coming west, but not the matter of which you speak. I want to ask you about Lilburn Boggs."

"The governor? What about him? He's dead, you know. Died six, seven years ago."

Pogue allowed he knew of the governor's demise and spent several minutes explaining the Boggs family's interest in the Missouri shooting and his assignment to make sense of the matter and, if only in their minds, finally put it to rest.

"So what I would like to know from you is, did Governor Boggs ever talk about his Missouri days and the shooting in particular? And, as well, I'm interested in anything else you know of the man, your impressions of him and such."

Harlan allowed as how it was a long story and that he had better have a cup of coffee before getting started. Pogue looked around the room as he listened to rinsing and rattling in the kitchen but saw nothing of interest. The dim room showed evidence of the woman who once kept it. The man sagged back into the room with a heavy china mug in hand, sat and had a sip, then pinched up his features in response to some unpleasantness.

"Cold," he said. "Must have let the fire go out."

Still, he took another sip, shoved around on the cluttered

tabletop to create a space for the mug, reached down and felt around between the chair and table, and fetched up a corked whiskey bottle with a few inches sloshing around the bottom.

"Reckon I'd best start at the beginning," he said as he splashed whiskey into the cold coffee. "This'll warm up my memory so's I get it right."

Harlan told how his widowed and remarried father had sent him from their home in Indiana, at age ten, to live with and work for an uncle. His guardian drove the boy hard, and by age sixteen he had, in his weakness, contracted consumption. With no need for a weakling lunger, the uncle passed Harlan on to another in Michigan. That family set out for California in the fall of 1845, wintering in western Missouri, just east of Independence.

"There were fourteen of us in the party, with eleven wagons—ten drawn by ox teams, one pulled by horses. First I heard of Governor Boggs was on the way to our winter quarters. When we was passing through Hancock County in Illinois, one of my young cousins fell out of a wagon, and it run over him. So we laid over for a spell not far from that Mormon kingdom in Nauvoo.

"They'd moved there after being run out of Missouri and was having considerable difficulties staying in Illinois. Seems they couldn't get along with their neighbors no matter where. Anyways, one of the things they was accused of—the Mormons—was shooting and nearly killing Boggs, who had lately been the governor who run them out of the state. That's the first I remember hearing about him."

Pogue made a few notes but found little of interest in what Harlan had to say. He laid the notebook in his lap and massaged his knee, trying to stay attentive to his host and hoping to hear something worthwhile.

Harlan kept talking, pausing only to nurse his coffee now and then. He told how his uncle circulated through the area during the winter months, asking about California-bound emigrants and learning where outbound parties would assemble come spring. Pogue perked up and took up his pencil again at the mention of Lilburn Boggs.

"We rolled out of Indian Creek in Kansas Territory early in April, in a train captained by Governor Boggs himself. Seems he'd recovered from his wounds sufficient to undertake an adventure, so was California-bound. There must have been nigh on five hundred wagons, some for California but most, two-thirds or thereabout, going to Oregon. We traveled together for a time, but then Boggs and the other men decided we would travel easier if we was to break into smaller groups. My uncle refused command of our train, so a fellow named Moran was elected. He proved incompetent and was soon replaced by Peter Inman, who claimed to be a preacher. Inman was worse, and him and me near shot each other when I tried to have him voted out. See, I was eighteen years old by then, and my health much improved, so I was counted among the men. Anyways, Moran got the job again.

"Squabbles over leadership wasn't unusual. Boggs's party did the same, voting the governor in and out of the leadership more than once, electing his son Bill to lead for a while, and sometimes putting some others in charge. The Reeds and the Donners did the same in their train. I suppose every company as ever crossed the plains did the same."

"Likely," Pogue interrupted quietly. "Tell me more about Boggs."

"Well, we only saw him from time to time, when the head men of each party had meetings to make sure things stayed even. We recruited for a while at Fort Laramie, and I saw him some then. Man at the fort said word was the Mormons was on the trail behind us, which didn't seem to make Governor Boggs any too happy. Seems like there was talk of reports in the newspapers back East, St. Louis or somewheres, saying the Mormons had sent out assassins to finish the job on Boggs. Destroying Angels, they called them, or Danites."

"Did Boggs believe it?"

"I think so. He sure enough seemed upset. Can't say as he was scared—he was a tough old gent—but it surely put him on his guard. He warned that Fort Laramie trader in no uncertain terms to keep an eye on the Mormons if and when they came through there. Claimed they'd rob him blind in any trade and steal whatever wasn't nailed down besides."

"Did he ever talk about getting shot?"

"Only in passing. Leastways in my presence."

"Did you ever hear him lay blame or accuse anyone of the deed?"

"No. Well, in a general way, I suppose—he left no doubt that it was the Mormons who was behind it."

"Think carefully now, Mr. Harlan. Did he ever mention the name Rockwell?"

Harlan sat quietly, the fingers of his right hand gently stroking the arm of his chair. Leaving off that idle task after a time that seemed to Pogue interminable, he picked up his mug to sip more of his concoction of whiskey and cold coffee and set it aside to rub his chin between thumb and finger.

"Might have. Once, maybe. Seems after one of the meetings one night, somewheres out along the Platte, Jacob Donner was asking him this and that about Missouri. I was talking with someone else—Frank Kellogg, likely—and only heard part of it. Overheard, I should say. But I guess I recollect hearing him say that name, then Donner asking if he was for sure the one and Boggs saying he was but could never prove it. Don't know that they were talking about the shooting, mind you. But that name, Rockwell, did come up, as I recall."

Harlan's next recollection of Boggs on the trail was at Fort Bridger. There they met one Lansford Hastings, who had written of a shortcut to California. Rather than following the Oregon road northwest to Fort Hall and branching off beyond there to the Humboldt River, Hastings recommended traveling due west from Fort Bridger to the Great Salt Lake, skirting its southern shore, and crossing the salt desert to reach the Humboldt, saving some three hundred miles.

Discussion and debate, argument and squabble divided the train over the subject, with Boggs opting to stay with the Oregon travelers on the familiar road until the trails split beyond Fort Hall. The Donners, Reeds, and Harlans took the advice and trail of Lansford Hastings. Yet another disagreement broke that train apart on the east slopes of the Wasatch Mountains—the argument being over the best way to get through those mountains. Harlan said that squabble resulted in the Donner-Reed party falling behind by several days, which delay ultimately led to their demise.

"That was a piece of bad luck for sure," Harlan said. "Our luck wasn't near that bad, but it was a far sight short of being good. Fact is, we only just missed finding our own selves in the same situation.

"I'll guarantee you that salt desert was horrible. But we finally made the crossing, having lost several cattle and a lot of supplies on the way. When we finally got to the Humboldt River, we learned that Boggs and his bunch had been through there days before. So much for that Hastings route being a shortcut.

"Anyways, as we was short of everything by then, my uncle gave me a poke full of money and sent me and Tom Smith ahead on horseback to see if we could buy some cattle and supplies in California and then backtrail them to wherever we would meet up again. We made our way along that sorry river quick as we could, sneaking past ornery Indians and fighting them now and then, and finally overtook Boggs.

"The governor allowed as we was doing a heroic work, and loaded us up with bacon and flour and such enough to make the trip. He also cached some along the river there, so as to replenish our party somewhat when they came along."

"Did he say any more about the Mormons? I mean, had he encountered any or had any word of them between then and when you last saw him at Fort Bridger?"

"Nary a word. Of course, we didn't really spend any time in idle talk. As soon as our horses was ready, we lit out again for California. Made it, too, and got all the cattle and supplies we needed through Captain Sutter.

"I saw Boggs again in passing on the return trip—which I made in the company of two Indians, as that contemptible Tom Smith abandoned me so as to go fight the Spaniards with Fremont.

Not that he cared anything about the Spaniards. Did it for money is all, twenty-five dollars a month.

"Anyways, I met up with Boggs again in Bear Valley, coming down the west slope of the Sierras. He was mighty glad to learn from me that the land ahead was every bit the paradise we'd heard of."

By now impatient, Pogue struggled to stay polite as Harlan described the remainder of his return journey and the narrow escape from the weather in getting across the summit above Truckee Lake where the Donner and Reed train met its fate only days later. And Harlan talked on, relaying in more detail than Pogue cared to hear, his subsequent adventures and misfortunes. The investigator stayed with him until he had the wagon train safely at Sutter's Fort.

"So, Mr. Harlan, is that the extent of your doings with Lil-burn Boggs?"

"Oh, no. Heavens no. I owe the most important day of my life to that man."

"How so?"

"Well, I spent most of the next year down south campaigning against the Spanish," Harlan said.

Oh no, Pogue thought. *Here we go again.*

"When I came back to these parts, the governor had been appointed *Alcalde* and was a man of some influence and responsibility. So when Ann Eliza agreed to be my wife, it was Governor Boggs who read out the ceremony and made it official.

"Twenty years ago, that was. Twenty years I spent with that woman," he said, reaching for whatever was left in the china mug.

———————◆———————

I suppose it was around about 1838 when the Missouri pukes came after us again. Our folks had spilled over into other counties, and other settlers were flockin' to the country, and sure as you don't feed sheep and cattle in the same pasture, them settlers didn't want to share none of the country with no Mormons.

Even some of our own was flyin' the coop, throwin' in their lot with the Gentiles—which was what we called them as wasn't Saints. Seems some Mormons admired our prophet from a distance but couldn't see nothin' but faults with Joseph there among us. Me, I knowed him and counted him for a friend for years, and I couldn't see no reason not to do as he counseled and make his every wish my command. Disloyalty don't set too well with me, so when our leaders came down hard on them dissenters, they had my support all the way. I even put my mark to a paper warnin' them traitors to get in line or get out.

Trouble is, they didn't want to do neither. What they did was run to the government for help, and with that Mormon-hatin' Lilburn Boggs bein' governor at the time, we figured they's likely to get it.

That's when Joseph give counsel to organize a company of loyal followers to herd them wanderin' fools back into the fold or drive them off. Sons of Dan is what we called it, but Danites is the name that stuck.

Doc Avard was appointed leader, and he took to the work like a willin' horse leanin' into a load. He wrote up a blood oath we all took, swearin' loyalty to our leaders, right or wrong, and offerin' to forfeit our lives if ever we faltered.

Some think Avard went too far. And, truth is, he did take the bit in his teeth and turned the whole Danite notion into a runaway. But even if maybe it did get out of control now and then, we did what needed to be done.

But punishin' our own traitors wasn't enough. Avard laid plans for the Danites to attack the Gentiles—who was givin' us as much trouble by then as they did back in Jackson County, maybe more.

They'd soon enough see trouble of their own.

EIGHT

Aboard ship

William M. Boggs
Napa, Calif.

My Dear Bill,
I take pen in hand to apprise you of my plans regarding our investigations in your behalf and also to help relieve the boredom I suffer aboard this ship. Since last we met, I have devoted all my energies to investigating your case. Following some interviews in the San Francisco area, I boarded a steamer home via the isthmus route, which I have since crossed and am now bound for New Orleans.
Upon arriving in Chicago, my intention is to spend some time with my family as well as my associates in the Pinkerton office. With their advice, I shall refine my investigative plans, but any deviation from what I outline here will be minor unless I miss my guess.
Nauvoo, Illinois, erstwhile home of the Mormons, is my first planned destination. After a brief visit there, I shall travel to Independence, where my inquiries are likely to involve several days. Thence, westward to Salt Lake City.
Depending on the outcome of those visits, it is altogether

possible that I will come again to you to present my conclusions. It is also possible, of course, that reasons for additional fact-finding will present themselves, requiring further investigation or following up with previous sources of information.

Until we meet again, I am your humble servant,
s/Calvin Pogue

Despite, or perhaps because of, the length of his absence, Pogue's reception at the family mansion was icy. Only Emily Elizabeth seemed pleased with his return, and her warmth alone kept the detective from catching a chill.

Again, his father-in-law summoned Pogue to his study, where, with appropriate solemnity, he reminded the detective of the error of his ways and invited—all but demanded—that he join the family business. With comparable gravity, Pogue again declined the offer. His wife applied pressure of her own, less stern but more intense than her father's. Only his mother-in-law ignored the subject. At least Pogue assumed so, since the woman did her best to ignore his very presence in her home.

He was pleased to learn, however, that Emily Elizabeth had been receiving the toy horses he sent home during his travels and that her stable was a sizeable one. During an afternoon together, he thrilled the girl with a horseback ride—on a brightly painted amusement park carousel pony that galloped in endless circles to the tune of a calliope. For, despite his sure knowledge that protecting her from the perils of actual horseflesh was overly cautious, Pogue chose not to further lower the temperature at home by disregarding the family's wishes in the matter.

Time at the Pinkerton office proved unfruitful. The voluminous clipping files contained no information—or even a folder labeled "Rockwell, Orrin Porter"—their contents limited mostly to bank and train robbers and outlaws of more recent vintage. So Pogue took to spending the bulk of his working hours huddled in

the morgue at the offices of the *Chicago Tribune*, studying clips
and files and back issues of correspondent newspapers from across
Illinois. The collection was incomplete but contained enough brittle, yellowed newsprint to strain his eyes for several days.

An item in the June 4, 1842 edition of the *Quincy Whig* caught
his eye:

NAUVOO, ILL., May 22d, A.D. 1842.
MR. BARTLETT —
*Dear Sir: — In your paper, (the Quincy Whig,) of the
21st inst., you have done me manifest injustice, in ascrib-
ing to me a prediction of the demise of Lilburn W. Boggs,
ex-governor of Missouri, by violent hands. Boggs was a can-
didate for the State Senate, and I presume, fell by the hand
of a political opponent, with his "hands and face yet drip-
ping with the blood of murder," but he died not through my
instrumentality. My hands are clean, and my heart is pure
from the blood of all men. I am tired of the misrepresenta-
tion, calumny, and detraction heaped upon me by wicked
men; and desire and claim only those privileges guaranteed
to all men by the Constitution and Laws of the United States
and of Illinois.*
*Will you do me the justice to publish this communication
and oblige?*

Yours, respectfully,
JOSEPH SMITH.

Pogue located the earlier edition of the *Quincy Whig* and
found the report Smith referred to in his letter.

*ASSASSINATION OF EX-GOVERNOR BOGGS,
OF MISSOURI*
*Lilburn W. Boggs, late Governor of Missouri, was assas-
sinated at his residence in Independence, Missouri, by an
unknown hand, on the 6th inst. He was sitting in a room
by himself, when some person discharged a pistol loaded with*

buck-shot, through an adjoining window — three of the shot took effect in his head, one of which penetrated the brain. His son, a boy, hearing the report of the pistol, ran into the room in which his father was seated, and found him in a helpless situation, upon which he gave the alarm. Footprints were found beneath the window, and the pistol which gave the fatal shot. The Governor was alive on the 7th, but no hopes are entertained of his recovery. A man was suspected, and is probably arrested before this. There are several rumors in circulation in regard to the horrid affair. One of which throws the crime upon the Mormons — from the fact, we suppose, that Mr. Boggs was Governor at the time, and no small degree instrumental in driving them from the State. — Smith too, the Mormon Prophet, as we understand, prophesied a year or so ago, his death by violent means. Hence there is plenty of foundation for rumor. The citizens of Independence had offered a reward of $500 for the murderer.

In the June 11 run of the same paper, the editor of the *Whig* reported the citizens of Nauvoo had voted a resolution "disapproving of the remarks of the Quincy Whig, in relation to the participation of Gen. Smith, in the violent death (he is not dead, by the way,) of Gov. Boggs of Missouri, and unanimously concurring in the opinion that Gen. Smith had never made such a prediction."

Pogue expected the news that Boggs had survived, despite initial reports, might bring an end to the newsworthiness of the event. He soon learned that was not the case. Mormons, their supporters, and their enemies seemed equally determined to keep the pot boiling.

In the *Warsaw Signal* of July 9, Pogue read a report quoting John C. Bennett, who said that "Mr. Rockwell started suddenly from Nauvoo, about two weeks before Boggs' assassination." Bennett, the report said, asked Joseph Smith where Rockwell was bound and was told "he had gone to Missouri to fulfil prophecies!" The assassin returned to Nauvoo, according to Bennett, and "the Prophet has presented said Rockwell with a carriage and horse, or horses; and he has suddenly become very flush of money, and lives in style."

This Bennett, Pogue decided from his reading, seemed determined to keep the heat on Smith, apparently using Rockwell as the match. That idea grew when he read in the July 16 *Whig* that despite threats on his life by Joseph Smith, Bennett would expose this "King of Impostors" and "consummate blackguard."

And, the newspaper said of Bennett, "He says that Smith prophesied the death of Boggs by violent means in 1841, in a public congregation at Nauvoo" and further blamed the foul fulfillment of that prediction on Rockwell.

Pogue carefully refolded the fragile newspaper. Smith's reported prophecy of Boggs's death, he thought, seems to have originated with Bennett. He returned the newspaper to the stack, massaged the itch out of his eyes with thumb and forefinger, and turned again to the dusty pile of unread newspapers. He found this in the July 22 *Quincy Herald*:

MORE TROUBLE BREWING

Gen. John C. Bennett passed through this city last Monday morning on his way to the Governor of Missouri, having in his possession the affidavits of a large number of the most respectable men, in and about Nauvoo, and in the county of Hancock, testifying that Joe Smith was the sole cause and instigator of the attempt upon the life of ex-Governor Boggs. Gen. Bennett says he is now determined to expose the whole mystery and imposition connected with Mormonism, and in particular will he bring to light the fraud, deception and humbuggery, which has enabled Joe Smith heretofore to maintain such absolute control over the minds and persons of his followers. The exposé will no doubt, be a curious and interesting document.

Bennett's trip must have given the Missouri governor ammunition to launch an attack. Pogue found an item in the August 14

Warsaw Signal reporting the arrest of Smith and Rockwell "in obedience to the requisition of the governor of Missouri. The charges upon which this requisition was founded, are those preferred by Gen. Bennett, viz.: that Smith was accessory & Rockwell principal in the recent attempt on the life of Gov. Boggs." Officers affected the arrest, the item reported, "but the prisoners were immediately brought before the municipal court of Nauvoo, on *habeas corpus* and discharged."

Pogue paged back through his notebook and found the names listed during his California meetings with William Boggs. He found the entry for John C. Bennett and then circled and underlined it. This man, perhaps, was more important to the story than Boggs intimated or perhaps knew, and he deserved further attention.

He'd have to look into it.

NINE

JOHN COOK BENNETT WAS, Pogue soon realized from his investigations, nothing more than a confidence man. He had seen the type before, but seldom one who accomplished what Bennett apparently did among the Mormons.

It seems the Mormon antagonist met Joseph Smith early in the history of his church but failed to see any potential in the prophet. Later, however, about the time the Saints established Nauvoo, Bennett saw opportunity and seized it. .

Despite a checkered past, of which Smith was aware, Bennett insinuated himself into the Mormon leader's confidence and into a number of prominent positions in both church and city.

But, it seemed to Pogue, Bennett's lust for power and control came to rival that of Smith's, and the two suffered a bitter parting. Just how much of Bennett's venom against his former friend grew from legitimate complaints, Pogue could not ascertain. His complaints and accusations could all be true, but he doubted it. It could just as easily be a pack of lies, but he did not consider that likely either.

In any event, he wanted to talk to the man. Maybe, these many years later, Bennett might be willing to tell the truth about what he knew of the assassination of Governor Boggs.

With help from fellow agents in the Pinkerton network, he learned that Bennett didn't stray far when he first left Nauvoo, living in various places in Illinois as he campaigned against the reputation of Smith and his Mormons.

After the prophet's murder, he formed temporary alliances with men vying for control of Joseph's church. Pogue learned that Bennett lived for a time with a disaffected Mormon sect on an island in Lake Michigan, but—much as he did in Nauvoo—wore out his welcome and moved on.

One false trail revealed nothing about Bennett but much about Mormon attitudes about Bennett, even as late as 1850. Brigham Young, by then firmly established as leader of the Church for life, told his followers that the greedy Bennett had gone whoring after gold in California and there met his demise.

Young claimed fulfillment of another Joseph Smith prophecy that Bennett would "die a vagabond upon the face of the earth, without friends to bury him," when, Young said, his body was "dragged out with his boots on, put into a cart, hauled off, and dumped into a hole a rotten mass of corruption."

But, Pogue found out, rather than going to the West Coast to die, Bennett had gone east to live—Plymouth, Massachusetts—where he was an abolitionist of some note. After the war, he relocated to Iowa. And, so far as the Pinkertons could learn, lived there still. The detective wrote, requesting a meeting.

Kornforth & Bowersox
Attorneys at Law
Des Moines, Iowa

Mr. Calvin Pogue
c/o Pinkerton Detective Agency
Chicago, Illinois

Dear Mr. Pogue:
Pursuant to your correspondence of the 6th ult. to our client John C. Bennett, we are saddened but obliged to say that Mr. Bennett died this past August. As our firm represents his estate, your letter came to us.

While unaware of the specific nature of the information you hoped to obtain from our late client, we ascertain from your missive that your inquiries revolve around his association with the Latter-day Saints. We are aware, from conversations with Mr. Bennett and our familiarity with his past writings on that subject (including a well received book, History of the Saints, a copy of which we have enclosed for your perusal), that there is some controversy surrounding that association.

It is also common knowledge that his conduct and character have been called into question by some, particularly the Mormons. We can only say that in all our relationships with Mr. Bennett, his integrity was of the highest order. This, of course, does not speak to his prior behavior, but we find it unlikely that the leopard, so to speak, could change his spots.

During his residence in nearby Polk City, Mr. Bennett earned the respect and admiration of his neighbors. He practiced medicine and was a sought-after surgeon, even here in the city, because of his early adoption of the anesthetic chloroform. He also made many strides in the field of gynecology.

Horticulture and animal husbandry were among his many hobbies, and his accomplishments in these areas may be likened to those of professional agriculturalists. His vegetable breeding experiments with tomatoes led to improved varieties. Professional journals published his papers on the breeding of chickens, and Mr. Bennett, in fact, developed several new breeds of fowl.

As a result, he amassed a not-insignificant fortune.

More important than money, however, was the esteem with which Mr. Bennett was held in his community of Polk City and surrounding areas, including here in Des Moines. He mingled with the highest strata of society, and his demise was mourned. He will be missed. At the same time, he is remembered with a suitable monument in the Polk City cemetery; perhaps the largest there.

We are sorry you will be unable to meet with Mr. Bennett as you desire. And, unfortunately, we are unaware of the presence among his effects of any information, beyond that which is already known, which can be considered likely to assist in your investigations or add to your knowledge of the late Mr. Bennett's sojourn among the Mormons.

We wish you success in your endeavors, and if you believe we can be of further service in your inquiries, we will do our best to comply with your every request.

With every consideration of respect,
s/Albert Scott Kornforth, esq.

The book the law firm included in the package was a copy of Bennett's *History of the Saints; or, An Exposé of Joe Smith and Mormonism*, published in Boston in 1842. Most of what Pogue found there mirrored the information found in newspapers and Bennett's affidavits. But the book, it seemed to the Pinkerton man, shed more heat than light on the subject.

The detective did find there a report of a conversation the author claimed he had with Rockwell. Bennett claimed Rockwell entered his parlor in Carthage uninvited and castigated him for spreading rumors about the Boggs affair.

"I've been told you said Joseph gave me fifty dollars and a wagon for shooting Boggs," Rockwell said. "I will whip any man who tells a cursed lie like that about me."

Bennett weaseled about saying it, as such, and asked if it was true that Rockwell had been in Independence at the time.

"Oh, I was there, all right. But if I shot Boggs, they have got to prove it. I never did an act I was ashamed of."

Then, according to Bennett, Rockwell left with this warning: "If you say that Joseph Smith paid me to shoot Boggs—I'll be back!"

———◆———

I weren't there myself, understand, so I can't swear to the whole truth of it, but what happened was told me by friends, and I tend to believe it.

There's this town in Missouri called Gallatin, on the Grand River up north in Daviess County where some of our boys went to vote on election day in '38. A bunch of them layabout Missouri pukes was there and vowed no Mormon would cast a ballot in that election. Our boys insisted, and the mobbers threatened violence.

Well, our boys wasn't havin' none of it. Someone of them flashed the Danite distress sign, and they lit into them pukes with fists, clubs, boulders—anything that came to hand. It was a fine fight, I'm told.

The mobbers ran to the law, or a judge, or some such. So a company of our Danites paid a visit to enlighten him, and to encourage him to take the side of those in the right—which, of course, was our Mormon boys.

Word got back to Governor Boggs that the Mormons was runnin' wild and terrorizin' the countryside and threatenin' the law, which was in no way true. If anything, it was us bein' terrorized. But Boggs called out the militia and ordered a shipment of guns sent to arm the pukes in Daviess County. He knowed, see, that there weren't many guns among the Mormons and figured he could put an end to us with some fast action.

Ha!

What that dumb man didn't know was that we caught wind of it and our boys waylaid them wagons on the road and made off with all them guns and the ammunition to go with them!

Word came down that Boggs was fit to be tied. But rather than lookin' into the situation to see who was in the wrong, he unleashed every militiaman and every mobbin' puke—all one and the same, if you ask me—in all Missouri, and declared open season on Mormons.

"Insurrection" is the fancy name for what he accused us of. "Protection" would've said it better. Whatever words you put to it, the dance had begun.

TEN

THE DISMAL MORGUE at the *Chicago Tribune* was, for all practical purposes, Pogue's home-away-from-home—his presence at "home" becoming increasingly uncomfortable—where he spent long, long hours.

It had also become a makeshift office, where he carried on his research while awaiting news of Bennett and refining his plans for pursuing other lines of inquiry.

His desk was an ink-stained table discarded by the newspaper's printers for storage in the cellar. The only illumination in the basement came from a pair of coal oil lanterns with soot-smudged chimneys. A rump-sprung wheeled chair proved so uncomfortable he spent a good deal of time standing hunched over the table, a stack of correspondent newspapers retrieved from bigger stacks around the room at his left hand. The current issue of interest lay spread before him, notebook open atop it to record any detail that appeared of interest.

The right side of the table held a careful stack of completed copies. Pogue welcomed the movement that restoring and replenishing the stacks afforded. Whether standing or seated, his knee throbbed with a dull ache most of the time, punctuated with occasional stabs of burning pain. Straightening the leg (as much as it could or would) upon arising from the rickety chair required a moment and several sharp breaths to accomplish. The dampness of the cellar didn't help any of it.

But the often histrionic newspaper reports were the most immediate source of information about events surrounding the assassination—attempted assassination—of ex-Governor Lilburn Boggs those years ago. The picture, while still something of a muddled montage, became ever more clear with the reading.

QUINCY WHIG
Saturday, August 20, 1842

> *The second attempt of Gov. Carlin, to apprehend Jo Smith and Rockwell, proved about as unsuccessful as the first. — When the officers arrived at Nauvoo, neither Joseph or Rockwell were to be found — they had either crossed the river into Iowa or were secreted in that holy city. . . . The whole affair begins to look exceedingly like a farce, and this opinion is becoming very prevalent. We suppose all proceedings will stop here for the present.*

It seemed to Pogue that three governors of two states—Reynolds of Missouri and Ford and Carlin of Illinois—had chased their tails in an effort to bring Rockwell and his prophet to justice for the attempted murder of Boggs. Another Quincy newspaper, the *Herald*, reported a third attempt in its September 8, 1842, number and commented on the failure.

"It is perfectly ridiculous that one man, of the calibre of Jo Smith, should throw defiance in the teeth of the people of two States. . . . For the honor of Illinois, we hope that effective measures may be speedily taken on the part of the governor to crush such treason."

Pogue read in the October 8 *Whig* that "Gov. Carlin has offered a reward of $400 for the apprehension of Joseph Smith and O. P. Rockwell, or $200 for either of them. It is not sufficient by $600 at least. A reward of $1000 might tempt the cupidity of the Mormons."

A postscript reported Smith in custody. But the October 15

edition retracted that: "JO SMITH *not* ARRESTED. — The rumor we spoke of last week, in relation to the apprehension of Smith, is not confirmed. We understand, however, that he was seen at Nauvoo on Friday last, apparently enjoying his liberty."

Further dusty newspaper stories in the morgue reported Smith and Rockwell on the lam for most of the rest of 1842. Reports concerning the more-prominent Smith were numerous, and it seems the prophet was hiding, more or less in plain sight, in and around Nauvoo. Rockwell's whereabouts were unidentified, but it was believed he had quit the Mormon stronghold for parts unknown.

Legal challenges from Smith's supporters led Illinois courts to first declare the Missouri warrant legal, then determine that it "lacked foundation." The controversy continued, with Smith finally hauled before the circuit court in Springfield in January 1843 for a hearing to determine whether or not he should be sent to Missouri to face charges related to the shooting of Governor Boggs.

A trip to Springfield seemed in order.

———————◆———————

Now I ain't sayin' I was there, and I ain't sayin' I wasn't. But there was one night when them Missouri pukes got a good idea of what the Danites was capable of. When the sun went down, there was three Gentile settlements standin'—Gallatin, Millport, Grindstone Fork—that wasn't there come sunrise.

Nobody was killed—folks was given time to get out. But roofs was pulled down, windows broke out, animal pens pulled apart, stock run off. And there was fires set. 'Most all of Gallatin was burned to ashes, and a goodly part of them other towns too. Some of our boys helped themselves to whatever possessions struck their fancy. Like Avard told us, "Take to yourselves the goods of the ungodly Gentiles."

About time them mobbers got a taste of their own medicine.

Not long after, another band of our boys went after a Missouri mob or militia or however you want to call it that was camped over on the Crooked River. As it was told to me, it was mostly a heap of confusion, with each side stumblin' over the other in the dark. One of the pukes was killed and a few Saints too. One we lost was David Patten—a heck of a fightin' man and leader. But the Danites drove them Missouri cowards from the field and set 'em to runnin' so our side called it a victory and went home.

Of course them cowardly excuses for militia soldiers ran cryin' to their friend Governor Boggs, who issued written orders to every militia officer and mob leader to drive all the Mormons out of Missouri.

Or kill us. Every one.

ELEVEN

THE RHYTHMIC CLACK and hum of wheels on rails lulled Pogue into a relaxed state somewhere south of wakefulness but short of sleep. An occasional glance out the window revealed only an ongoing monotony of the fertile farm fields of central Illinois.

Leaving Chicago yet again was not a pleasant prospect. Missing Emily Elizabeth's growing-up years grated on him. More and more, the joy of his daughter's presence seemed to overwhelm, or at least counter, his otherwise cold and unpleasant home life. The whole situation begged serious consideration.

Sometime.

With appreciation for the comforts of modern travel, he propped his bum leg on the seat opposite. His pending trip to the distant West spawned less anxiety than in the past, as he knew the steady creep of the coming transcontinental line would allow train travel to somewhere west of Cheyenne, if construction reports in the newspapers proved accurate.

Four hundred and some-odd miles in a stagecoach to complete the journey to Utah Territory would be no picnic, but immeasurably less taxing than the 1400-mile horse-drawn journey it once was.

But, for now, his destination was Springfield, Illinois.

Calvin Pogue grabbed his knee to shift the leg to a more comfortable position, leaned against the window, and set his thoughts adrift as the train rolled on toward the capital city.

The nameplate on the desk behind the counter read Owen Bradley. The man with that name sat slumped behind the desk, green acetate eyeshade knocked askew by the folded forearms on which his head rested.

Pogue stood in the doorway for a moment listening to the man snore. Gilt letters on the frosted glass of the propped door read:

CLERK
CIRCUIT COURT of the UNITED STATES
DISTRICT of ILLINOIS

Owen Bradley stirred at the sound of Pogue's knuckles rapping the countertop. He sat upright, massaged his sleep-smeared face with the palms of both hands, pulled a handkerchief from a pants pocket, and sponged rivulets of drool from creases on either side of his mouth. He returned the cloth, straightened his visor, and turned his attention to the man watching him at the counter.

"Help you?"

"I hope so. Are you Owen Bradley?"

"The same."

Pogue pulled his billfold from an inside jacket pocket and flipped it open to display his credentials.

"I am Calvin Pogue, with the Pinkerton Detective Agency."

"Pinkerton man!"

"Yes, Mr. Bradley. I'm hoping for your assistance with my current investigation."

"And just what do you mean, 'assistance'?"

"If I might sit down, sir, I'll be pleased to lay it out for you. But I am afraid the situation is somewhat complex."

The clerk got up, lifted the hinged end of the counter, and invited Pogue into his sanctum, waving him into a side chair near the desk. Pogue told Bradley about his case, eventually getting around to his wish to see the records from the January 1843 trial of Joseph Smith.

"As it happens, I remember it well," Bradley said. "I was a court reporter back then, and still wet behind the ears. That was my first big trial. So I not only know the records you're asking about, I took them down in shorthand and copied them out for the record."

Pogue glowed in his good fortune. He knew the judge and principal attorneys involved in the case—the only names he knew—had all died, and he had figured his odds of finding anyone familiar with the case would be slim. But here, in the person of Owen Bradley, was a man who had heard every word spoken in open court, transcribed every affidavit, every motion, every precedent cited. And he had entered the judge's ruling and supporting opinion into the record—which was, Bradley told him, boxed up and stored in a warehouse on the outskirts of Springfield.

Bradley offered to go himself and fetch the case files and then meet the agent two days hence with the records he sought. And, he said, he would arrange his schedule to help Pogue read the transcripts and pass along his recollections of the once-notorious trial. "Not much happening here just now, what with the court out of session."

Pogue shook the clerk's hand and conveyed his appreciation for the effort, then left the courthouse for the room he'd taken at a nearby hotel.

———◆———

"You would not have believed that trial," Bradley told Pogue once they'd settled in at the clerk's office for what the Pinkerton man assumed would be a long day. "Not like a normal proceeding at all."

"How do you mean?"

"It was more like a circus or carnival," Bradley said. "There was Mormons in town thick as alley cats on a dead rat. A whole army of them had escorted Joe Smith to town, along with the county sheriff who arrested him, and they all stayed around for the trial—to see he got justice, they said, but more likely to take him away by force of arms should things turn out not to their liking. Some of his head men—'apostles,' as they called them—were here, and officers and soldiers from their Mormon militia, women with picnic lunches, kids, dogs, you name it. All here fully expecting to see their prophet exonerated.

"Same time, there were Mormon haters by the score—here for the opposite reason, of course. They'd been trying to get the goods on Joe Smith for a good long time and saw this as their main chance."

Bradley opened a folio and withdrew a stack of papers pinned together. Pogue noted the heading:

CIRCUIT COURT OF THE UNITED STATES
FOR THE DISTRICT OF ILLINOIS
Before the Hon. Nathaniel Pope, Presiding Judge

"Now ol' Judge Pope—there was a man," Bradley said. "He knew his law but had his own way of conducting court.

" 'Most every day he sat for trial, he'd invite some of the city's finest young women to join him on the bench. 'Angels,' he called them. Claimed they lent a touch of class to the proceedings. A distraction they were, more likely. Least to my way of thinking.

"Smith's trial was no different. Bevy of beauties lined up beside Judge Pope. Mary Lincoln among them. Young Abe had a law office here, back then. Up on the second floor. I don't recollect his being in town at the time, but his bride surely was a witness to the proceedings that day."

Fetching a pair of spectacles from a vest pocket, Bradley wrapped the hooks behind each ear, positioned them on his nose with a forefinger, and turned his attention to the court record.

"See here. Says a writ of habeas corpus was issued for Smith on the thirty-first of December, 1842, demanding Sheriff Wilkin of Sangamon County bring Smith, who was in his custody, before the court.

"Then, see, here's the warrant from Governor Thomas Ford ordering the arrest of Smith."

"For what cause?"

"On account of this," Bradley said, running his finger down the page. "Here's a warrant from Thomas Reynolds, governor of Missouri. Says, 'I, by these presents demand the surrender and delivery of the said Joseph Smith.'"

"But not Porter Rockwell?"

"Strange enough, no. Because see, here, earlier on, he says:

"'Whereas, it appears by the annexed document, which is hereby certified to be authentic, that one Joseph Smith is a fugitive from justice, charged with being accessory before the fact to an assault with intent to kill, made by one O. P. Rockwell'—see, there's your man—'on Lilburn W. Boggs, in this State, and it is represented to the Executive Department of this State, fled to the State of Illinois.'"

Pogue asked, "But it doesn't ask for the arrest and delivery of Rockwell? Only Smith?"

"That's right."

"Do you remember why?"

"No. I expect maybe because folks in Missouri was more interested in reeling in the big fish. Not too worried about the trigger man so much as the man who handed him the gun."

"What about here, where it talks about 'the annexed document'?"

Bradley turned to the next sheet. "This," he said.

STATE OF MISSOURI / COUNTY OF JACKSON

This day personally appeared before me, Samuel Weston, a Justice of the Peace within and for the county of Jackson, the subscriber, Lilburn W. Boggs, who being duly sworn, doth depose and say, that on the night of the sixth day of May, 1842, while sitting in his dwelling in the town of Independence, in the county of Jackson, he was shot with intent to kill, and that his life was despaired of for several days; and that he believes, and has good reason to believe from evidence and information now in his possession, that Joseph Smith, commonly called the Mormon Prophet, was accessory before the fact of the intended murder; and that the said Joseph Smith is a citizen or resident of the State of Illinois; and the said deponent hereby applies to the Governor of the State of Missouri to make a demand on the Governor of the State of Illinois, to deliver the said Joseph Smith, commonly called the Mormon Prophet, to some person authorized to receive and convey him to the State and county aforesaid, there to be dealt with according to law.

s/LILBURN W. BOGGS

Sworn and subscribed before me, this 20th day of June, 1842
s/Samuel Weston, J.P.

"No mention of Rockwell," Pogue said.

"Nary a word."

"As I understand this, then, Boggs recorded his suspicions with this justice of the peace, and on the basis of those suspicions, demanded that the governor of Missouri demand that the governor of Illinois arrest and extradite Smith."

"That pretty much sums it up."

"And all this came about in the summer of '42. But the arrest and trial didn't happen until December and into January. Seems I read about some earlier attempts to arrest Smith and Rockwell—even Smith being caught a time or two, then released."

"Right. All he had to do, see, was have the courts in Nauvoo—which, like everything else in that city back then were under his thumb—issue a writ of habeas corpus, then they'd spring him."

"Those earlier arrests, too, were based on these same papers from Missouri?"

"As I recall."

"Governor Ford finally brought him in. Why not Carlin? 'Most all this came about during his term."

"Oh, but he was a lame duck and, I suppose, mostly didn't want to be bothered. He demanded both Smith's arrest and his release at different times, if memory serves. Finally, he more or less washed his hands of the whole situation. Left it for the newly elected Ford. Of course there were plenty of folks who claimed it was because Governor Carlin supported the Mormons, but I don't know about that."

Pogue studied the papers, wondering why both governors accused Rockwell of the crime in their documents, when Boggs did not mention the name in his sworn statement.

He suspected, as well, the hand of John C. Bennett was stirring things up somewhere in this whole business.

After a sleepless night spent kneading his scarred knee, medicating for pain with whiskey, and wandering the quiet streets of Springfield, Pogue waited for Bradley when the man unlocked his office door.

The clerk allowed Pogue to peruse the records at his leisure, coming and going as he dealt with other duties around the courthouse. But he made it a point to tell the detective about Joseph Smith's counsel at the trial, Justin Butterfield.

"Oh, he was a wit, that one, and a fine lawyer. He was United States district attorney at the time."

"A federal prosecutor, acting as defense attorney?"

"Yes. It is an oddity."

"So who prosecuted the case?"

"Oh that was Josiah Lamborn, Attorney General of Illinois. Anyway, about Butterfield. He stood up on his hind legs to make his argument before the court and bowed to Judge Pope.

"'I rise to address the Pope . . .' he said. Then he bowed to the ladies there on the bench with him and said, 'surrounded by angels.'

"Then," Bradley said with a smile as he pointed out the lines in the transcript, "he turned to his client and the Mormon contingent and said, 'in the presence of the holy apostles, in behalf of the prophet of the Lord.' That brought down the house, I'll tell you.

Judge Pope gave his gavel a good workout to restore order in the court. And he, himself, laughing the whole while."

Pogue smiled at the tale, but more at Bradley's delight in the telling. When the clerk left to take lunch, the investigator read through the record carefully enough to get a sense of the proceeding while looking for information about Rockwell. The name was not mentioned until near the end of Pope's opinion. The judge simply noted the inconsistency of Rockwell being blamed for the crime in the Missouri governor's demand, but not in the sworn statement by Boggs.

Not much to go on.

Pogue buttonholed the court clerk when he returned from his dinner break.

"Mr. Bradley, I thank you for your time, your patience, and your cooperation. Before I leave you to your duties, please help me understand the judge's ruling."

"Of course."

"As I read this, he set Smith free primarily because Joseph Smith had not committed any crime in Missouri. The crime Missouri claimed he did commit, that of being an accessory in the attempted murder of Boggs, occurred—if it did—in Illinois. Yet they wanted to try him for it in Missouri. Have I got it right?"

"That pretty well sums it up," Bradley said. "Pope wouldn't buy the idea that Smith was a fugitive from justice in Missouri when no one ever claimed he'd committed a crime or fled from arrest there. And, as it says there somewhere, the judge found a number of flaws in the paperwork from Missouri."

"So do you think justice was done?"

"How do you mean?"

"Do you believe Rockwell tried to kill Boggs and that Smith put him up to it?"

Bradley mulled that one over for a moment.

"I can't rightly say. Times were pretty tense, them days. Lots of violence around Nauvoo, both against and by the Mormons.

"I suppose it's possible. I don't know much of Rockwell, but I know he had a reputation as something of a ruffian. But he never set foot in this courtroom and, as you've seen, was barely mentioned in the trial.

"Guilt or innocence aside, I think the judge was right in determining that the case made by the State of Missouri was a fraud. No right-thinking court would send a dog to the pound on such skimpy evidence so poorly presented."

The Pinkerton man again expressed his appreciation to the court clerk.

Tomorrow, he'd take the mail coach to Nauvoo and see what, if anything, he could learn thereabouts.

———————◆———————

It wasn't but a couple days after that battle at Crooked River and Boggs's extermination order when the Missouri militia took its revenge.

There was this little town—if you could call it that—called Haun's Mill, where a couple dozen Mormon families lived. Most of 'em came there from Ohio and hadn't even homes. Livin' out of their wagons, they was, sleepin' and cookin' in the dirt.

They's just mindin' their business one day when the militia rode into town with guns blazin'. The women and little ones run off into the woods and hid. The menfolk forted up in a blacksmith shop and fought them off best as they could with what few guns was at hand and what little powder and ball they had.

Them pukes just kept pressin' and 'fore you know it they was gunnin' down the Mormons in that buildin' like they was fish in a barrel. Killed eighteen men and boys. One of 'em wasn't no more'n ten years old. Some brave soldier put a gun to his head, looked him in the eyes, and blowed his brains out.

They's all killed or run off from Haun's Mill—just like Boggs ordered.

TWELVE

THE STAGECOACH ROLLED DOWN Nauvoo's main street in a cloud of dust, which settled as the team slowed and stopped in front of the wagon yard. Pogue opened the door and hopped out gingerly, favoring his right leg, the ride having rendered his left knee more stiff and sore than usual. Once his feet felt firm under him, he arched his back, reaching behind with both hands to massage the hollow above his buttocks.

He removed his hat and used it to slap the dust from his pants legs and the front of his jacket. At the driver's call from up top, he turned and caught his carpetbag, stepped onto the boardwalk, and walked toward a hotel two doors down. As he crossed the mouth of an alley next to the stagecoach line's stables, a rhythmic tappety-tap-tapping caught his ear.

Pogue located the source of the sound partway down the alley. There, next to the side door of the stable, a man sat on a keg of some kind. He held a straight stick in his left hand, on the end of which was a crude wooden horse, maybe six inches tall, pieced from carved blocks. The toy had jointed legs, held together with loops of twine, and the hooves tap danced on a long, thin, narrow board—something like an oversized shingle—between the man's legs, cantilevered under his backside. Pogue watched for a moment, seeing that the clattering dance of the hooves was caused by the fingertips of the man's right hand tapping out a rhythm on the board, causing it to bounce lightly against the loosely hinged legs of the horse, which flopped back and forth and "tap danced."

Curiosity accompanied Pogue down the alley. Other than a glued-on mane and tail of the same twine that hinged its legs, a dot of black paint for each eye, and hooves blackened from a dip in the paint pot, the dancing horse was unadorned. Its color was that of the light-colored wood it was cut from—a claybank dun.

Following a brief conversation and a bout of bargaining, Pogue left the alley with the pony and platform tucked under his arm.

———◆———

Twenty and more years after being abandoned to the mobs of Illinois by the Mormons, Nauvoo was still mostly deserted. Once the state's largest city outside of Chicago, it was now little more than a ghost town. Many of the homes and buildings put up by the Saints stood, some occupied and others abandoned and empty. Still others, including the holy temple on the hill, were burnt-out skeletons.

But the town wasn't dead yet. A few hundred people, some of them Mormons who could not or would not follow Brigham Young west, still farmed the area and scratched out a meager living from business ventures.

Among them was Emma Smith, Joseph's widow. Now married to a man named Bidamon, she still lived in the "Mansion House," built during her time as the prophet's wife as a hotel with family living quarters—though its days of taking in lodgers were long gone.

The woman who answered Pogue's knock at the Mansion House was severe looking: gray-shot, dark hair drawn back and knotted at the nape in a bun so tight she appeared stretched to the toes, high-collared dress buttoned at the neck with cuffs drawn tight around her wrists, dark eyes sharp and penetrating as she examined her caller.

"Yes?"

"Ma'am, I am Calvin Pogue—an investigator with the

Pinkerton Detective Agency of Chicago. Perhaps you have heard of us."

"Yes, I suppose I have."

An uncomfortable silence followed, during which the woman's face betrayed nothing.

Pogue shifted his feet, took off his hat, and said, "I wonder if I might come in. I have a few questions I would like to ask you."

Another lengthy pause. Then, "I cannot imagine what I might know that would be of interest to the Pinkertons."

"It concerns the attempted assassination of Lilburn Boggs, former governor of Missouri. I'm sure you remember."

Finally, after giving the detective another once-over, the woman said, "That was a long time ago."

This time, it was Pogue who stretched the silence.

"I guess you may as well come in. Lord knows my neighbors have fodder enough for gossip without seeing me passing time on the porch with a strange man."

Once inside, the woman's demeanor changed—she was, in fact, pleasant of personality, good humored and agreeable. She offered coffee, which he accepted, and invited Pogue to join her in the kitchen. "It's so much brighter than this stuffy old front room."

She was right. Large windows on two walls of the big room admitted sunshine, filtered through shade trees growing thick in the backyard. A trestle table sat in the corner with spindle-back chairs on two sides, placed for the view.

"Tell me what you remember of that time," Pogue said, once Emma placed cups of coffee and a plate of cookies on the table and sat.

Emma sipped her coffee and nibbled at a cookie while formulating an answer. "Hard times," she finally said. "The good people of Missouri had run us out, making us leave behind all we owned. We had no choice. Governor Boggs and his infernal 'extermination order' left us no alternative.

"I have no doubt his constituents would have carried out his order and killed us all had we not fled. By the thousands. Even though Illinois agreed to take us in, we were in disarray. Once

Joseph was freed from jail and joined us, things got better. We acquired this town site and, with hard work and the Lord's help, flourished for a time.

"But," she continued after another nibble of cookie and sip of coffee, "it wasn't long before the persecution began anew."

"I know your husband—late husband—was accused of complicity in the shooting of Boggs."

"Then you also know he was cleared of any involvement."

"I understand you were present at the court proceedings."

Emma laughed. "Indeed. Me and half of Nauvoo, it seemed. Saints packed the courtroom, filled every window, and stood tight as broom straws in the doors and hallways. The rest—the most—spread quilts on the lawns of downtown Springfield and had a picnic. Quite a time, that."

"The affidavits from Missouri—one of them, anyway—said Orrin Porter Rockwell shot the governor."

"Folks said Porter did a lot of things. From what I hear, blame is still laid on him for every foul deed in the West."

"But do you think he might have done it? He was in Jackson County at the time, from what I've learned."

"More coffee, Mr. Pogue?"

"Thank you, no."

Emma gathered the cups and the cookie plate and carried them across the room. She slid the remaining cookies into a china jar decorated with painted flowers, then pumped water into the cups and left them in the sink.

"Porter did come back to Nauvoo not long after the reports that Governor Boggs had been shot," she said, wiping her hands on her apron before sitting again.

"We thought for a time Boggs had been killed, but later the papers said he lived through it. No one here was sorry to hear of his death, and no one here was happy to hear he had lived. No man ever did more wrong to the Saints.

"But, to answer your question, I don't know if Porter did it or not. He might have. He was certainly capable of it. And, had he thought or even imagined that Joseph wanted it done, he would have done it."

"Did Joseph want it done?"

Again, Emma laughed. "You had to know Joseph. Despite all Governor Boggs had done, and despite the fact that Joseph would not have spat upon the man had he been on fire, the Prophet would not have harmed him. To a fault, Joseph was kindhearted and wished no one harm."

"Rockwell knew him well? Joseph, I mean."

"He did. Porter knew Joseph long before I did. They knew one another since they were boys. Porter was some years younger—ten or so—and looked up to Joseph. Hero worship, if you know what I mean. Followed him around like a puppy. So he knew Joseph's disposition.

"But Porter's was somewhat different. He was a gentle boy, but what we went through in Missouri turned him hard. Short-tempered, he was, and sometimes acted before he thought about what he was doing. You must understand about Porter that he was—is—one of the most capable men I have ever known. Anything he set his hand to, he could accomplish.

"However, he was not, if you catch my meaning, a deep thinker. Not simple-minded, but simple. He had no guile. He assumed others were the same. When he felt wronged and got his blood up, he dealt with the situation as he saw fit. Decisively, sometimes violently."

"Did you talk to him—or hear him talking to your husband—when he came back from Missouri that time?"

"No, not really. Just the usual. You know: Hello. Good-bye. Can I get you something to drink. That sort of thing."

"Where did the notion that he shot the governor come from?"

"That part of it is easy. John Bennett. He stirred up all manner of rumors. Cast aspersions, spread innuendo—and it went lots farther than just Porter and Joseph. But as for Porter shooting Governor Boggs—there were plenty of folks willing to believe it, Porter being Porter and all. But be that as it may, there never was a true word that came out of the mouth of John C. Bennett."

THIRTEEN

ONCE AGAIN, POGUE FELT disappointment that there was no opportunity to question John C. Bennett. The fallen Mormon leader, it appeared, was the string that held this case together, knotted and tangled and twisted though it might be. The Pinkerton man could only hope that more information, from whatever sources his inquiries turned up, would unravel the tale.

Maybe what he had yet to learn from Emma Smith would help.

"Bennett's claims were what cast suspicion on your late husband Joseph and laid the blame on Porter Rockwell as well."

"That is true. Never mind that it was all lies. John Bennett was a fast talker and made his living convincing people to believe any number of outlandish things. Some believed what he said about the Boggs affair. Enough to make a peck of trouble."

"Where was Rockwell while all this was going on—the arrest and the trial in Springfield?"

"Joseph and Porter laid low after the Nauvoo courts freed them the other times. Joseph hid out here in town, sometimes across the river. Porter went east when things got to looking bad for him. Pennsylvania, it seems. Not long after Judge Pope turned Joseph loose and told the State of Missouri to leave off, Porter tried to come home.

"But some bounty hunters saw him on the boat landing in

St. Louis and captured him. They jailed him in Independence. Kept him locked up for months. His treatment could not have been good, for when he finally came home, he was in sorry shape."

"Why was he released?"

"They had no evidence. Not even enough to put the poor boy on trial."

"Yet you say they held him for months."

"I don't recall exactly when they caught him. Springtime, it seems. Nor do I know the day they turned him loose. But I will never forget the day he got home."

Emma lifted the apron from her lap to wipe away moisture that filled her eyes.

"Christmas day, 1843, it would have been. Joseph and I were hosting a party, in the great room here at the house. Most of the Church leaders were in attendance, friends and neighbors from here in Nauvoo. Fifty invited guests, there were. Food, drink, dancing, you know the sort of thing.

"There was a disturbance. One of the gentlemen guarding the door—we were always on the lookout back then—came to Joseph and told him a man was trying to come in and would not be denied. Said he looked like a tramp, unwashed and foul. Drunk, perhaps. Joseph went into the front room to investigate, and I followed. He took one look and told the guards to throw him out.

"But the man spoke, and Joseph took note. They stared at one another for a moment, and then Joseph laughed and embraced him. 'Orrin Porter Rockwell!' he said. 'You have come home!'"

"For all practical purposes, the party was over after that," Emma said. "At least for the men." She told Pogue they gathered around Rockwell, filled him with wine, and listened to stories of his imprisonment.

"The poor boy. As he told his story, we could only thank the Lord that he survived. The law in Independence kept him much of the time in a cold, damp cage in the cellar. What passed for food wasn't fit for the slop bucket. Much of the time he was chained so close he could neither rise nor recline.

"When they finally freed him, he walked more than two

hundred miles through the dead of winter to get home. And that mostly at night, for there were wicked men watching for him every step of the way, bent on his destruction.

"That day, that Christmas, was the occasion of a prophecy by Joseph that has since become legend. Porter, you see, was crowned with the most disgusting mop of hair and beard you can imagine. Long and tangled, matted and crawling with vermin. God only knows why, but Joseph laid his hands on Porter's head and blessed him; told him that if he was faithful, and if he left his locks unshorn, his enemies could never harm him.

"Porter kept that covenant for as long as I knew him, and, so far as I know, has kept it ever since. His long hair and beard became a badge of honor to him, and soon became a sign of warning to others. But why Joseph thought to turn him into a Samson, I do not know. It must have been, as he said, God's will for Porter."

From that time forward, Emma said, her husband felt, more than ever, an obligation to Rockwell. He attempted to establish him in business and set out to build a combination saloon and barber shop in Nauvoo. But something had to be done while it was being built, so Smith opened a bar in the Mansion House and asked Porter to run it.

"That was a mistake," Emma said. "One I put right at first opportunity. It happened, you see, in my absence or it would not have happened at all. I was in St. Louis at the time, purchasing furniture and fixtures for this place. It was unfinished, you see.

"The first thing I saw when I came home was that the front room had been outfitted as a barroom! There were several townsmen sitting about imbibing, and Porter serving them from an inventory of spirituous liquors and keg beer.

"Joseph heard my thoughts on the matter right away. 'But Emma,' he says, 'a hotel needs a bar. And Porter needs a job.' I told him none of that mattered a whit. It was unseemly under any circumstances for a prophet of the Lord and leader of a religion to be engaged in devilish enterprise, I said. I told him it was his decision, but if that bar stayed in my house, the children and I would not."

Pogue did not have to ask what happened. The steel in Emma was plain to see. She said that afterward, Rockwell became Joseph's bodyguard and was seldom out of arm's reach. Some said Porter killed at Joseph's request.

"But you don't believe it," Pogue said.

"Nary a word of it. They accused Porter of slitting people's throats, drowning folks in the river, shooting them, and all manner of evil. I will never believe Joseph would order such a thing."

"But Rockwell must have earned his reputation as a killer somehow."

"I'm not saying he did not kill. As I have said, those were hard times. Violent times. We were under attack from mobbers most of the time, and for many in Nauvoo, it came down to kill or be killed. Porter was caught up in any number of altercations where self-protection—and the protection of others—became necessary. As it happened, his skills in those circumstances were considerable, and he managed to outlive his attackers.

"And while it has been many years since I have seen Porter, the stories I hear from out West lead me to believe it has been so ever since."

After her husband's murder, Emma said Rockwell, like most of the Mormons, opted to follow Brigham Young. He continued his work as a bodyguard and became as loyal to the new Mormon leader as he had been to Joseph.

"I have heard that Porter is still accused of killing on orders of Mormon leaders. With Brigham Young in charge and no law to answer to out there in the desert but himself, I do not doubt it.

"That man—Brigham Young—has been the ruination of Joseph's church."

With a trip to Salt Lake City drawing nearer by the day, I may well find out soon enough, Pogue thought as he bid Emma Smith Bidamon good-bye.

———◆———

Most of us Mormons had already flocked into Far West by the time all them folks was slaughtered at Haun's Mill. There was thousands of us there. Strength in numbers is how Joseph figured it, and we put together a sizeable force.

Our Mormon militia and the Danites was at work buildin' up fortifications around the town and spyin' on the enemy. I scarce remember how many nights I slept in my boots.

Of course every Missouri puke with a gun in hand beat a path to Far West as well. Them militiamen marched on us but called a halt when they saw our battle line outside of town. With three hundred or so soldier-Saints, we had 'em outnumbered. And, as Joseph said, we had right on our side. We'd give them mobbers a hard time, he told us, and angels would fight by our sides.

So the pukes pulled back into the woods. But they kept showin' up in numbers till a day or so later there was three mobbers to every Mormon. Then word came down to us about that massacre at Haun's Mill. Joseph must have decided them angels wasn't in a fightin' mood.

After that, he weren't neither.

He and some others went out meanin' to parley with the militia officers, and they took him hostage. With Governor Boggs on their side, them so-called soldiers wasn't in no mood to parley with no Mormons.

They kept Joseph and them out there on the cold ground all night long, threatenin' to slaughter 'em ever' minute. We stayed on the line till mornin', ready to attack or defend ourselves, whichever. But it was over. Word came back from Joseph to give it up. Some wanted to light into 'em anyhow, sayin' our prophet had betrayed us and the Lord.

But, like always, most of us stuck by Joseph.

If that weren't enough, they rigged up a court martial and convicted Joseph and them others of treason and sentenced 'em to die by firin' squad in the town square of Far West. Thank God for Alexander Doniphan. He was a militia general of some sort at the time, and it was him that was ordered to have Joseph shot.

But he wouldn't do it and said he'd see that anybody who did would be punished for carryin' out illegal orders.

So they chained up Joseph and hauled him around the countryside in a wagon like it was some circus freak show, lettin' any and *every puke what cared to, to heap insults on him and pelt him with stones and such. He eventually ended up in jail in Liberty, down in Clay County.*

Boggs had us right where he wanted us. Disarmed. Defenseless. Most of us didn't even care anymore if we did die. But that excuse of a governor didn't back off an inch. He was determined we'd be pushed out of Missouri, so he had his mobs keep pushin.'

FOURTEEN

BEFORE QUITTING the Nauvoo area, Pogue traveled the twenty or so miles south and east to the county seat at Carthage. He hoped to talk to someone in the sheriff's office there and get another opinion of Porter Rockwell.

Upon learning at the courthouse that the sheriff was out delivering a summons but expected back at any time, he wandered the town square. An old man sunning himself on a bench pointed out the Carthage jail, scene of Joseph Smith's murder. The smallish two-story building was a jail in name only, lacking security of any serious sort, but had served as a lockup in days gone by.

His impromptu guide pointed out the second-story window from which the bullet-riddled Mormon prophet had fallen, and the well against which he had been propped to die.

"We got that Joseph Smith, all right. Him and his brother. It's a shame we didn't kill every one of them Mormons. I was among the Carthage Grays that shot them two, and proud of it. Didn't make it up the stairs to fire any of the lethal bullets though, and sorry I wasn't. Every day since I've wished I had been. Bad luck. But I was there, and I saw that conniving lunatic get what was coming to him."

Pogue did not question him further, believing any information the old man might offer would be tainted with hate to a point beyond credibility. Fortunately, just then a horseman rode through the square and tied up at the courthouse rail.

"Would that be the county sheriff, by chance?" Pogue asked.

"That's him, all right. Worthless piece of junk."

Pogue thanked the man and hurried over to the courthouse. "Sheriff!" he called as the man climbed the steps.

The lawman stopped and turned to watch the stranger hobbling toward him.

"Yes?"

"A word, sir, if I might," Pogue said. He stiff-legged it halfway up the steps, stopped just below the sheriff, and extended his hand. "Calvin Pogue."

The sheriff shook the offered hand, his grip firm and steady. Pogue guessed the man's height at near six feet, maybe more, his estimate distorted by the stairs that separated them. Decked out in workman's dress rather than the office attire so many men of his rank chose, the tall man's clothing started with riding boots at the bottom and topped out in a dusty bowler hat. Just under its short, rolled brim, a pair of heavy eyebrows bristled, which, like the thick mustache that grew below a generous nose, were nearly white, tinged with fading red. Pogue noticed the strap of a shoulder rig inside the man's jacket and saw the badge pinned to a shirt pocket.

"Yes?"

"I am with the Pinkerton Detective Agency of Chicago."

"I am unaware of any railroad banditry in my jurisdiction," the sheriff said with a slow drawl. "Fact is, I am unaware of much in the way of railroads here at all."

Pogue laughed. "I can assure you, sir, that the Pinkertons have interests other than the railroads. Not many, I'll grant you. But my business lies elsewhere."

"Have a seat, Mr. Pogue," the man said and grabbed his pants legs by the thighs, hitching them up as he lowered his long frame and sat on the steps. Pogue stepped up to the officer's level, turned, and, with some difficulty, sat down, extending the inflexible leg in front of him as he did.

"The war?" the sheriff asked, with a nod toward the leg. Pogue nodded in the affirmative.

"My name is Rutherford C. Fargo, sheriff of Hancock County. Rutherford's a bit of a mouthful, so make it Ford. How can I help you?"

"Well, Mr. Fargo—"

"Ford."

"Ford. I am looking into the attempted assassination of Lilburn Boggs, a former governor of the neighboring state of Missouri."

"I know the name. A little late, aren't you?"

Again, Pogue laughed. "True. But Governor Boggs died out in California not long ago, and his family wants to know, once and for all, who shot him. He forbade any inquiry while alive—out of fear, they say—but now he is not around to object, and they intend to find satisfaction. And I have been engaged to provide that satisfaction."

"And just how do you suppose I can help?"

"I wonder if you—or anyone in an official capacity you can direct me to—was around at that time. My hope is to learn something of the people involved, or said to be involved."

"I suppose I'm your man. Leastways, I was here back then, serving as a deputy to Jacob Backenstos."

"What became of him?"

"Well, J.B. came to be mighty unpopular on account of all that business with the Mormons. He was elected sheriff in about '45, but it got so hot around here for him that he joined the army in '46 to go fight in that Mexican War. Fighting Mexicans seemed relaxing by comparison to being here, I guess. Don't rightly know what he did after. Heard tell he went off to the Oregon country and finally drowned himself in a river. Leastways, that's what's said. But I don't know."

"Who ran him off?"

"That would be the fine citizens of Hancock County. Believed J.B. to be in league with the Mormons, they did."

"Was he?"

"Not to my way of thinking. The sheriff was a fair-minded man. He had no particular sympathy for the Mormons or their ways but figured they was getting a raw deal. He encouraged them to fight back, see, and there were plenty of folks around here who didn't like that.

"Also, J.B. would arrest anyone he saw breaking the law, no matter who. Some people thought they had a right to just help themselves to anything that belonged to the Mormons and didn't appreciate being called to law for thieving. Nor did they think it was the sheriff's business to be rousting them for burning out Mormons and beating on them and such. J.B. thought it *was* his business."

"What about you?"

Fargo said, "I just kept my head down and did my job. Followed the sheriff's lead but didn't make a big deal of it. Me being a deputy saved me from blame, I guess. Folks laid it all on J.B."

"And you came to be elected sheriff."

"It took a while. Once the Mormons were run off, things mostly calmed down. All but the most ornery—like that old fart on the bench over there—just let it ride. I guess I ended up where I am because I outlasted everybody else."

Pogue shifted his seat sideways and propped his game leg on a higher step. "The name I hear most often associated with the shooting of Governor Boggs is Orrin Porter Rockwell. Did you know him?"

"Yes, I knew Port. 'Most everybody did. And them that didn't, knew of him. And feared him."

"What was he like?"

"Smallish guy. Shorter than average and narrow of frame save a barrel chest. Had these tiny little hands, delicate-like. High-pitched voice that would get to squeaking when he was agitated. Then there was that long hair of his.

"But don't get the idea he was girly in any way. And God help the man who would say such a thing in his presence. He was harder than an anvil and able to take as much pounding. He could stay up days and nights on end, sharp-eyed and alert the whole time. And I'll tell you, Port could shoot."

Asked for an example, Fargo told of a time when Sheriff Backenstos was driving on the Warsaw Road one fall morning and spied three horsemen and two others in a wagon. He recognized one of the riders as a decided Mormon-hater—a man named Frank Worrell, who led the militia mob that killed Joseph Smith—and suspected they were up to no good.

His guess must have been a good one, for the minute they saw the sheriff, they set out after him, figuring finding him alone on a country road offered a good chance to get rid of him. Backenstos whipped up his team but was losing ground. He topped a hill, and the road dropped down to a stream crossing.

As it happened, Porter Rockwell and a companion were stopped there, dismounted and watering their horses. The sheriff reined up in a cloud of dust, told the men of his predicament, and deputized them on the spot to protect him.

"J.B. told me that Port pulled his rifle from its saddle scabbard and stepped into the road, cool as summer lemonade," Fargo said. "About that time, Worrell and another rider topped the rise, having left the buckboard and other rider behind in the race.

"The sheriff hollered out at them, and they stopped a hundred, maybe a hundred fifty yards away. J.B. told them to leave off, but Worrell drew his pistol.

"He never had a chance to fire. Porter Rockwell cut loose with his rifle and hit his target square in the belly, even at that distance. They said the shot knocked Worrell out of the saddle and tipped him head over heels off that horse's rump, and he hit that road like so many pounds of lightning-struck sheep.

"'Bout that time, Worrell's wagon showed up. They tossed his body in the back, wheeled around, and drove away from Rockwell's smoking rifle like there was a pack of rabid wolves nipping at their heels."

Scribbling furiously in his notebook as Fargo told the story, Pogue dotted his final sentence and then asked, "Based on what you know of Rockwell, do you think it's likely he shot Boggs?"

"Wouldn't put it past him," Fargo said, stroking his mustache with a thumb and forefinger. "Only there's just one thing."

"What's that?"

"A man that can shoot like Port wouldn't have missed. I believe

Boggs would have been toes up under the Missouri dirt all these years if Rockwell had taken a notion to kill him."

———————◆———————

Whilst Joseph and them was in that dungeon in Liberty, Brigham Young and some of the other head men in the Church did their best to get thousands of Saints out of harm's way in Missouri. They scouted around and cut a deal with Illinois, so it was to the east we went.

The courts and Boggs kept tryin' to trump up some charges against Joseph. Then Avard, who run the Danite bands, turned tail and blamed it all on the Prophet.

I rode with the Danites from the start, and it was Avard's show all the way. Not that we was reluctant to do Avard's bidding, mind you. There was plenty of us more than willin' to do all he asked and more. When it came to punishin' them mobbin' pukes, we was eager to do it anyway we could. But Joseph, he was only in the background on all that stuff, and so far as I know never lifted his own hand—not in no Danite oath, and not against any man in the whole of Missouri.

Anyways, gettin' folks ready to move and movin' 'em out of that cesspit called Missouri weren't easy, I can tell you that. Dead of winter. Boggs's deadline for us to be out of there was April of '39.

We hadn't enough of anything, from teams to wagons to food— most didn't even have no shelter from the weather, what with the mobbers havin' burned or busted up everything we owned. I spent days workin' with stock, gettin' horses trained to the harness and brea- kin' cattle to the yoke. There was whole crews of men tearin' apart busted-up wagons and cobblin' together new ones and makin' carts out of the leftover pieces.

Durin' them times too, I was packin' messages back and forth to Joseph. And it weren't just words I was carryin', I can tell you. Them men would've starved, most likely, if I hadn't managed to rustle up some scarce grub from time to time.

I also sneaked in some tools so's they could sneak themselves out of that hole. They tried bustin' out once when the trap door was lifted for visitin' day. They got out of the hole, all right, but the jailers just locked 'em in the upper part of the jailhouse so they got nowhere.

One other time, though, they nearly made it! See, they had nothin' to do but sit all day, so keepin' up a steady attack on them walls weren't no hardship. I'd smuggled 'em in some strong augers and drill bits, and they went after them walls like they meant it. Which was a job, I'll tell you, as them walls was double-built of thick timber, with rocks and boulders fillin' the gap between. They was nearly through the whole mess but had worn out or broke all the auger braces.

So I rustled 'em some new handles for them drillin' tools, but I got caught smugglin' 'em in. 'Course that alerted them jailers to the scheme, so that plan went bust. It cost Clay County a pretty penny to repair that jail though, I can tell you that!

We got most all the Mormons who wanted out of Missouri over to Illinois by Boggs's April deadline, diggin' in at a place called Quincy on the Mississippi River. Not long after, Joseph showed up. This was still in April of '39, if I recollect proper.

Whilst they was movin' him and the other prisoners to another jail after some business with the courts, someone of them Missouri big shots realized they weren't goin' to be able to pin nothin' on Joseph, so the guards just let them all escape. They sure could've saved us all and themselves a passel of trouble had they just left him alone in the first place.

I don't know who decided to let them get away. It might've been Boggs himself. If it was, it was the only smart move that fool ever made.

FIFTEEN

THE RIVERBOAT MANEUVERED into the dock at St. Louis, and Pogue waited on deck while the crew positioned the gangplank. He stepped onto Missouri and paused to look around, realizing he stood at the more-or-less exact spot where the bounty hunters captured Porter Rockwell.

From here, shackled hand and foot, the gunman had been hauled across the state by stagecoach and incarcerated in the Independence jail. The detective mused on the irony of the name for a moment, and then set out to post a letter and a package.

On the Mississippi River, Quincy, Ill. to St. Louis, Mo.

A. Pinkerton
Pinkerton National Detective Agency
Chicago, Ill.

Sir:

My inquiries in Springfield, Nauvoo, and elsewhere in Illinois are complete and, I am reluctant to say, of limited value. It appears that most memories revolve around the larger circumstances and events surrounding the shooting of ex-Governor Boggs rather than the incident itself. Opinions and ideas on the matter are as disparate as the people who offer them.

I am, as I write this, steaming down the Mississippi toward St. Louis, at which place I shall disembark and proceed to Independence by rail.

Since I have so little of value to convey, I have determined not to report to our client, William Boggs, as yet. My expectation is that more relevant information will come to hand in Independence, and I will write Mr. Boggs following my investigations there. Should Mr. Boggs inquire, please be so kind as to inform him that he will be hearing from me soon.

My detailed notes and analysis concerning the case are recorded in my notebooks, which are available for your inspection at any time you wish. But, as I said before, there is, to date, little of worth—although I am getting something of an idea of the events of 1842, which information will, I trust, prove vital in the course of my investigations as they proceed.

I am, as always, your respectful and obedient servant,
s/Calvin Pogue

P.S. I have enclosed expense reports and receipts &c. &c. to cover my travels since last being at the office. Please, if you will, deposit additional funds by wire to a bank of your choosing in Independence and inform me by telegram, care of the city police there, where the money is waiting.

Nauvoo, Illinois and elsewhere

My Dear Emily Elizabeth,

I enjoyed immensely our time together while I was at home. It breaks my heart to be apart from you, but my work takes me away, and so I must go. Please mind your manners and obey your mother in all things, as she wants only the best for you.

Here I am sending you a most unusual steed. He is not fancy to look at, I admit, but you will, I am sure, find him an enjoyable companion. Once you have put him through his paces, you will understand the odd way in which he is put together.

Let me tell you what to do with this horse (he does not have a name so far as I know; please give him a suitable one).

This I am about to tell you will prove difficult for a girl in a dress, but I am sure you will work it out. The thing to do is arrange your skirts so you can sit on a chair with the end of the long board under you so the rest of it sticks out between your legs as if you were on a short seesaw. Hold onto the stick and set the pony lightly on the far end of the board, so it only just touches. Then, with your other hand, tap gently on the board.

You will see the horse dance! With practice you will soon have him dancing as fast or slow as you wish, and you will learn to tap out different "tunes." (I know this, as I have tried it myself!) Please teach this pony a few dances and be ready to put on a little program for me when next I am home.

Until then, all my love and highest regards,
Father

———————◆———————

For the next few years we—Luana and me and the youngsters—mostly stayed around Nauvoo. That's where we went after Quincy. Joseph moved the Saints to this godforsaken bog upriver a ways. Then he turned it into as fine a city as ever there was. Grew to be about the biggest place in all Illinois.

Made a trip or two back to Missouri over the next few years on account of Luana's folks still bein' there. But we came and went pretty quiet, Mormons still bein' subject to ill treatment and it bein' rumored around that I had been among the Danites.

But mostly I stuck pretty close to Joseph in them Nauvoo years.

Bodyguard, I was. We took a journey to Washington to see the President, Joseph wantin' Missouri punished, or leastways to make some payment for the Saints' losses there. Late October, early November it was—I recollect on account of leavin' just a day or two after my boy Orrin was born. Nigh onto six months, we was gone that time. See, I ended up nursemaid for old Sidney Rigdon, who took sick on the journey, and he and I never made it to Washington. Met up with Joseph afterward in Philadelphia.

It turned out Van Buren was like most other connivin' politicians when it came to dealin' with Mormons—told Joseph to forget about any help from him or anyone else in the government.

Bounty hunters and lawdogs from Missouri was sniffin' around Nauvoo most all the time, wantin' to get their clutches on Joseph for escapin'. Boggs just wouldn't leave off. Illinois wouldn't offer nothin' in the way of protection. Fact is, one time Joseph walked out of a meet with Governor Carlin and got arrested by a couple of deputies. We never seen it comin'. Ended up in the high court of Illinois, that one. But they sprung him on account of Missouri not havin' any legal warrant to hold him or have him shipped back to Missouri for trial.

Still, Joseph weren't none too happy with either one of them governors. He spoke prophecy that Carlin would die in a ditch. And that Boggs would die bloody within the year.

SIXTEEN

THE HOUSE SAT ALONE at the end of Spring Street, a quiet lane well away from the busyness of Independence. Tall trees shaded the one-story clapboard home that seemed to Pogue modest quarters for an ex-governor.

He studied the house, the road, the woods, and the public spring that sat opposite the house and gave the street its name. Then he walked through the yard and up the front steps and knocked on the door. While awaiting an answer, he pulled the billfold with his Pinkerton credentials from an inside pocket of his jacket. A young boy—he looked to Pogue to be four or so—opened the door. He said nothing, only looked up from under flaxen eyebrows at the man at the door.

"Is your father at home?" Pogue finally asked.

Still silent, the boy turned and disappeared into the house. After what seemed several minutes to the Pinkerton man, the boy returned with a man, his father, in hand.

"Can I help you?" he asked, eyeing his visitor suspiciously.

Pogue held his identification out for the man to see. "My name is Calvin Pogue. As you see, I'm an investigator with the Pinkerton Detective Agency. I'm here on a case and hope you will indulge me with a bit of your time."

"And how do you suppose I can help?" the man asked, looking as uncertain as before.

"Is this the home where Lilburn Boggs, once governor of the state, lived?"

"It is. But that was long ago."

"My investigation concerns events from that time. Our agency is looking into the attempted murder of the governor. I'm wondering if you are aware of that incident."

"Sure. The people who had this place before us told us all about it. I think they may have bought the house from the Boggs family when they left town. Then again, maybe not. You could check the title down at the courthouse, but I guess that doesn't matter much. Anyway, I only know what the people here before said when we got the house."

"Can you show me the window through which he was shot?"

The boy followed his father out the front door, and Pogue fell in line down the steps and around the corner of the house. A brickwork chimney split the side of the house, and beyond it a window punctured the wall. It looked to be about two feet wide and twice as tall, muntins splitting it down the middle and dividing it crossways into eight panes of glass. A wooden sill extended outward from the window a few inches. Bushes grew against the house and away from the wall a foot or so.

"May I?" Pogue asked with a nod toward the window.

The man nodded his permission, and Pogue stepped up and peered into the window. The room beyond was still in use as a sitting room, with a settee and a number of upholstered chairs bordering an open, central area. Lamps rested on a few side tables, and a tall bookshelf with cabinet doors on the bottom sat against one wall.

The homeowner stepped up next to Pogue and said, "They said the governor had an overstuffed chair he sat in to read his newspaper of an evening. As I understand it, it sat a couple of feet inside this window, facing the center of the room but angled a bit toward where that bookcase sits. Sort of like where that wooden chair sits. Makes sense, I guess. That way, someone sitting there could take advantage of the light from the window, or maybe a cooling breeze. Of course he got shot at night, so there would've been a lamp lit. Don't know where it would have been."

"I'm told there was a young girl and a baby."

"So they say. From what I understand, they were on the floor in front of the governor's chair."

Pogue studied the scene. It was likely, he decided, if what the man said was true, that the youngsters would have been hidden from the assailant. Whoever fired the shots, Pogue preferred to think the assassin was unaware of their presence.

"Several balls—a dozen or so—peppered that wall opposite," the man said. We replastered the wall a few years ago, and the pockmarks were still visible. They'd been filled before, but you know how plaster has a way of sinking into holes. Anyway, I suppose the lead is still under there, stuck in the wood."

Pogue walked around the side yard, studying the window from various angles and distances. He looked in other directions as well, considering escape routes. The visit was helpful. A good place to start. But he knew the place might have changed some over the years. And it would certainly present a different picture in the dark. Heavy rain, like the storm of the night in question, would likewise alter the scene. The investigator couldn't order up a cloudburst, but he could certainly count on regular occurrences of nightfall.

"I appreciate your letting me look around. I would like to see it after dark one night. Would you mind if I returned, perhaps in the company of someone who was here at the time, a policeman or the like?"

"Not at all. Just knock at the door, so the wife and kids don't take a fright."

With a handshake and a reaffirmation of his appreciation, Pogue took his leave. As he walked the quiet street toward the more settled parts of town, he wondered if he followed the footsteps the would-be assassin walked those many years ago.

———◆———

Early on in '42 Luana was gettin' close to birthin' another baby and wanted to go to her ma's to do it. So we booked passage on the riverboats to Independence.

Not where I wanted to be, by any means—but you know how women is.

"Mr. and Mrs. Brown" was the name we gave. I found work with a man by the name of Ward who had a high-priced stud and some other fine mounts. My job was carin' for and workin' with them horses.

Along about May, Boggs got his head blowed to bits.

Missouri didn't seem a safe place to be, what with the ex-governor dead or dyin', so I kissed the wife and little ones good-bye and made it back to Nauvoo.

SEVENTEEN

THE JAIL IN INDEPENDENCE was easy to find. The imposing two-story brick structure sat in the middle of the block, set back from the street only by the width of a narrow sidewalk.

The front door opened onto an enclosed reception area, so small as to feel confining. A man behind a wall with a window cut in it eyed Pogue suspiciously when he entered. "Help you?" he asked.

"I'd like to ask about a prisoner."

"Name?"

"Rockwell. Orrin Porter Rockwell."

"Doesn't sound familiar," the man said and started paging backward through an oversized register book on the counter below the window.

"It was a long time ago. I don't think you'll find him in there."

The jailer looked up, puzzled. "How long ago?"

"1843."

"Nope," he said, closing the book. "He won't be in here. Matter of fact, you won't find him anywhere."

"How's that?"

"Well, see, this here jail was built in 1851. Old jail burned down. Along with all the records."

It was Pogue's turn to look puzzled. "All gone?"

"Every page. Sorry."

Pogue turned to go but stopped at a question from the guard. "Mind if I ask what's your interest?"

"I'm a Pinkerton man. I'm investigating—if that is the right word, given that the incident occurred so long ago—the attempted murder of Lilburn Boggs, who was once governor of this state. A man suspected of the crime was held here. In the old jail, rather."

"I think I've heard something of that shooting. Maybe. Way before my time, I'm afraid. I've only been here in Independence—Missouri, for that matter—since the war ended. Sorry."

Again, Pogue turned to go. But the disappointment hanging on his face must have moved the jailer.

"Hold on. You need to see ol' Joe Reynolds."

The name sounded familiar. The sheriff, he remembered. Reynolds had been sheriff in Jackson County when Rockwell was jailed here.

"Sheriff Reynolds? J.H. Reynolds? He's still around?"

"Sure thing. He's justice of the peace. Has been for years. Nearly forever, they say."

Pogue made it out the door when he turned to go this time. But this time he held a scrap of paper from the jailer. He had written an address on it, sketched a crude map, and explained in unnecessary detail how to get to the justice's office.

———◆———

Joseph H. Reynolds leaned his considerable bulk back in his desk chair while Pogue explained the situation and outlined the information he hoped to obtain.

From time to time the old man snorted scornfully. He held a rumpled handkerchief and mopped his brow regularly with a mechanical motion that suggested more habit than necessity. Eventually, his eyes glassed over, his forehead furrowed like a plowed field, and the handkerchief worked in earnest. Finally, he leaned forward with a squeak of the chair and aimed a wagging index finger at his guest, the handkerchief waving like a flag of surrender.

"Enough! Listen here, Mr. Pinkerton man. The last thing I want to do is dredge up Lilburn W. Boggs and them Mormons. Those people were responsible for the most miserable period of my entire existence so far on God's green earth. You show up here out of the clear blue sky spitting out names like Joseph Smith and Porter Rockwell, jabbering about affidavits and indictments and arrests and escapes, and it gives me the chilly quivers just to hear the sound of it. But just to make sure I've not gotten addled in my declining years, tell me again what you want to know. And why."

Pogue laid it out for him. Realizing the error of his initial approach, he omitted the questions he wanted answered and simply said he had been engaged to investigate the assassination attempt and to try to fix blame, and would appreciate any help he could get.

"Boy, we couldn't pin that shooting on anybody when it happened. What kind of unbridled arrogance makes you think you can do it all these years later? With all due reverence, of course, for the extraordinary powers of the Pinkerton Detective Agency."

"Mr. Reynolds, I do not wish to impose on your valuable time. But since it is altogether likely that you know more about this crime and its aftermath than anyone, I will be grateful for anything you can tell me. Perhaps if we could meet under more congenial circumstances. Might I buy you lunch, or maybe dinner? Could we meet later for a drink? Mr. Reynolds, sir, I am at your mercy."

———◆———

Boggs didn't die. The ornery man survived wounds that would've killed most anybody, from what I was told.

Boggs bein' Boggs, him and his cronies soon enough started lookin' for a Mormon to blame. Someone who knew my name wasn't "Brown" told of seein' me around Independence, so I was accused. While they was at it, they added Joseph to the list, claimin' I did it under his orders.

We was both of us arrested in August, our own governor havin' set the law on us on account of some legal paperwork he got from Boggs. They wanted to send us down the river and into Missouri, but the law in Nauvoo put a stop to that, sayin' them papers from Boggs wasn't legal in Illinois. So they locked us up in the Nauvoo jail, and we was walkin' the streets again soon as them deputies left town.

Well, I couldn't see waitin' around for 'em to come after me again, so I left town. I figured they'd soon enough forget about me. Instead, they put a price on my head. Missouri offered more'n a thousand dollars for my capture! And it would go up higher yet, if you can feature such a thing!

I should've turned myself in. Could've used the money. See, I spent the next eight, nine months a stranger, wanderin' across Indiana, Ohio, Pennsylvania—who knows where all—starved out and lookin' for work that wasn't to be had. That little tour cost me my wife too. Luana cast me off as a poor proposition for any kind of future. Can't say's I blame her, I guess. But it sure didn't make life any easier.

Finally, I said to heck with it and figured I'd go back and see if she'd give me another go. Missed her and them children somethin' awful.

That proved to be one more bit of bad judgment on my part.

I no sooner stepped off the boat in St. Louis than I felt a gun barrel in the small of my back. Man said not to move and to keep my hands where he could see 'em. The reward on me by then was three thousand dollars, he said, payable whether I's dead or alive. Said it didn't matter much to him either way.

Well, it mattered to me. So I went along with his suggestion.

EIGHTEEN

THEY SAT DOWN to lunch together at a small café around the corner from the Justice's office. He was hesitant to talk at first, but once he got used to the idea, Joe Reynolds was actually invigorated by rehashing the past and the attempted assassination of Lilburn Boggs. Dredging the muck of his memory was slow and cumbersome at first, but words eventually washed over Pogue in a steady stream that soon ran at flood stage.

"Came here in 1834. Independence back then bore no resemblance to the peaceful settlement you see here today. Place was more like an anthill after a hatch, and stayed that way every spring and summer for years.

"The streets were crawling with Mexicans coming up the Santa Fe Trail and herds of bullwhackers going down the trail. Indians of all kinds everywhere. Fur trappers talking bastardized French, English, Spanish, and who knows what all. Negro slaves and white-boy dayworkers totin' loads in every direction. Buyers, sellers, and traders dealing in anything and everything you can imagine. Folks with all their possessions stuffed in greenwood wagons organizing into companies to emigrate to the Oregon country.

"There were flatboats unloading, freight wagons and pack trains loading. Docks down on the river backed up three deep. Every road and street crowded and chaotic. Fights breaking out over every spot that emptied out either place. So many cusswords flying through the air they made a haze.

"Dust on the ground so deep you'd wonder if you'd ever stop sinking before you bottomed out somewhere above your ankles. And mud—oh, yes, the mud. We'd get a good gullywasher, and it'd turn that dust into the stickiest mud ever invented. Deeper than the dust, it was."

Through all this, and more, and more still, Calvin Pogue sat silent. His notebook and pencil rested on the table before him, as useless as the greasy dinner plate and smeared flatware that lay next to it. The lunch sat heavy on Pogue. Given the nature of the food served, the obvious pleasure Reynolds took in it, and the quantities he took in, Pogue understood the man's girth.

Reynolds told that he'd been elected justice of the peace in 1837 and had held the office pretty much ever since. He'd served terms in the state legislature on a couple of occasions. But it was his successive terms as county sheriff, from 1840 to 1844, that interested the detective. He asked about them.

"Running for sheriff didn't seem like such a bad idea at the time. And the first term wasn't so bad. The Mormon troubles was pretty well over with by then. Them fanatical folks had been run out of Jackson County back in '33. Then they caused all that trouble up north in Clay, Caldwell, and Daviess Counties and got run out of there. Governor Boggs saw to that.

"Anyway, last thing I expected was havin' to deal with them golden-bible-thumpin' lunatics. Turned out that's about all I did deal with them last two years of wearin' that badge. From here to Illinois, I tried to mop up the messes them fool Mormons made."

"I would very much like to hear about that, Mr. Reynolds. Perhaps we could meet later for drinks."

"Why not. Instead of drinks, let's make it dinner. What say we meet here this evening about seven o'clock?"

"Seven it is."

"See you then. I've wasted this much time on this sorry tale. I might as well see it through to the end."

———◆———

The battered satchel hit the table with a dusty thump. Reynolds dragged a chair well out from the table and settled his bulk into it with a grunt. He shook out a handkerchief and mopped his brow, puffing loudly to catch his breath.

"Found this old thing between the wall and a cabinet," he said, waving the hanky toward the cracked leather bag. "Knew it was somewhere. Stuffed some papers in there during my sheriff days. Might be something of interest; leastways something to jog my memory. We'll get to it once we've et," he said as he eyed the dinner selections on the chalkboard on the eatery's wall.

Pogue ate only a small portion of the meatloaf he ordered. After a few reluctant bites, he spent his time pushing the rubbery glob back and forth across the plate, smearing trails through the pasty gravy, and then mashing the overcooked string beans into mush and spinning his fork in the lumpy mashed potatoes. Even the keg beer was warm and flat in its filmy glass. The swarm of sticky flies circling the table, unresponsive to any amount of swatting or swishing, did nothing to improve the investigator's appetite.

His guest, however, tucked into a massive platter of fried liver and onions as if it would be his last meal for a good, long while, using slice after slice after slice of white bread—dried out almost to the point of qualifying as toast—as a backstop for his busy fork. The string beans seemed to his liking as well, for he asked the waitress for a second helping as she refilled his buttermilk glass for the third time.

The waitress finally carried away Pogue's plate and swished a stained mop rag around the table where it had sat. He watched Reynolds continue his attack on the slimy mess on his plate for a few more minutes and then said, "May I?" with a nod toward the briefcase.

Reynolds nodded his approval without missing a stroke of his vigorous chewing.

Pogue tugged at the tarnished buckle on a stiffened leather

strap riveted to the flap over the front of the bag, eventually freeing it. Inside he could see a jumble of papers, apparently thrust into the case with no thought for order or organization. He slipped the two-inch stack out onto the tabletop and tapped the edges to straighten the pile somewhat. After examining each sheet, he set it aside, creating an adjacent pile. Most of the papers appeared to be personal in nature but related to the sheriff's duties—letters, receipts, lists of things to do, copies of reports, that sort of thing.

An official-looking document caught his eye. The top of the page read:

STATE OF ILLINOIS, LEE COUNTY

At the bottom:

Sworn and subscribed before me at Dixon, this 29th day of July, 1843.

FREDERICK R. DUTCHER, Justice of the Peace for Lee County, Ill.

Pogue read a few paragraphs and realized it was an affidavit related to a "Statement of facts connected with the arrest of Joseph Smith and his discharge therefrom" and attesting that Joseph H. Reynolds "did peremptorily refuse to allow Smith a private interview with his counsel" for at least an hour, "until after being informed by at least two of these deponents that such private interview must be allowed Mr. Smith as that was a right he had guaranteed to him by law." The affidavit was signed by seven men. Pogue did not recognize any of the names.

The next paper in the pile was similar; an affidavit sworn the same day before the same justice of the peace, this one signed by three of the same men as the other. Here, they stated "under oath" that they traveled with "Joseph H. Reynolds, the agent of the State of Missouri, from Dixon to Nauvoo, at the time he had Joseph Smith in custody with the intention of taking him to Missouri" and that "friends of Mr. Smith" met on the journey and in Nauvoo "made use of no means of intimidation towards said Reynolds; but, on the contrary, pledged themselves that said Reynolds should be personally safe."

Pogue found himself confused. The document also said that Reynolds had been arrested and disarmed by the sheriff of Lee County.

"What is all this?"

NINETEEN

"THAT, MR. POGUE, was the most ridiculous sideshow you can imagine!" Reynolds said, sitting upright, dropping knife and fork and slamming the heels of his hands to the table. "Not even on the stage of a troupe of traveling actors have I ever seen such a farce!"

The ex-sheriff shoved the flatware aside, pushed his plate away, tore the napkin from his collar, and dabbed at his mouth with energy enough to fell a man of smaller stature. He tossed the napkin onto the tortured remains of his dinner, yanked a handkerchief from his pocket and attacked his glistening brow with vigor. Once he regained his composure, he launched into the tale.

Reynolds gave Pogue to understand, first of all, that the position of sheriff of Jackson County was an elective office. As such, the man who served was at the beck and call of politicians and, if the officeholder had political aspirations, had better serve their interests. Everyone from the governor on down, including legislators, mayors, councilmen, commissioners, and party hacks of every variety had considered him their personal errand boy.

"See, after Boggs got gunned down and everyone finally settled on that scoundrel Porter Rockwell as the trigger man, the die was cast. Rockwell was a Mormon, and that meant Joseph Smith, and that's who they wanted to swing for the crime. If a Mormon did it, then Smith had to be behind it—them Mormons lacking any ability to think or act on their own."

And so it was that with Rockwell in custody, men with political influence demanded that Reynolds go to Illinois and arrest Smith and bring him back to Independence for a speedy trial, conviction, and execution. Boggs made a sworn statement that he believed Joe Smith was behind the crime, the governor of Missouri wrote up a warrant demanding the governor of Illinois arrest Smith as a fugitive from Missouri justice and turn him over to the Jackson County sheriff.

So, in June of 1843, off went Reynolds to Illinois. In Nauvoo, he learned that Smith and his wife were visiting relatives and preaching near the town of Dixon in Lee County, some two hundred miles upriver and inland.

"Ask me, he somehow got wind we were coming after him and had slunk off like an egg-sucking dog. I gathered up a local constable from Hancock County and went after him. Arrested him. Knocked on the door of the house where he was staying and asked to see 'Brother Joseph.' Simple as that. He came to the door, and I shoved a gun in his guts and told him he was my prisoner and was bound for Missouri.

"But then some of Smith's cronies convinced the Lee County sheriff we were kidnapping Smith—and he arrested us before we could get out of town!

"The whole parade started for the county seat, from where I intended to take Smith down the Illinois River to the Mississippi, on down to St. Louis, and up the Missouri to Independence. The Mormons in Nauvoo somehow got wind of it, or figured out what we were going to do, and sent a boat up the Mississippi from Nauvoo loaded with some of their militia to intercept us.

"We changed plans. Smith, who me and that Hancock lawman had under arrest, and the Lee County sheriff, who had the two of us under arrest, all started overland for Quincy, where we intended for Judge Stephen A. Douglas himself to sort out the whole mess. Of course I had no intention of getting there—I planned to get that Mormon moron across the river to Iowa or Missouri or anyplace else that wasn't Illinois at first opportunity."

That plan, too, went astray. Along the road, still a hundred or so miles shy of Quincy, everyone who was under arrest and everyone who had arrested everyone else met up with an army of Mormons.

"Joe Smith laughed when he saw his boys coming and allowed that he wouldn't be going to Missouri this time. I figured I was a dead man, and that's the God's truth. There were nigh on to two hundred ornery Mormons in that bunch, every one of them ready and willing to burn a hole through me with a smoking ball of lead.

"Of course Smith never wanted to go to Quincy any more than I did, the great Stephen A. Douglas being no friend of the Mormons, so the whole mess of us caravanned to Nauvoo. They turned it into a celebration, and we were the parade. Brass band and the whole works."

The Lee County sheriff who had arrested Reynolds and the Hancock County constable who helped Reynolds arrest Smith all went before a judge in Nauvoo.

"That judge there—if you could call him such a thing—was under Joe Smith's thumb. So, of course, he declared Smith a free man, thanked the Lee County sheriff for rescuing his prophet from our evil clutches by arresting us, and sent him on his way. Then he freed me and the man from Hancock County who helped me arrest Smith on condition that we get out of town and leave the holy man alone forevermore."

Pogue listened to the story, biting his lip most of the time to restrain unwelcome laughter.

"So what about these affidavits?" he asked once he felt confident of his composure.

"Oh, them. Well, they don't amount to nothing. Just them Mormons' lame response to newspaper reports about that sorry affair. Trying, after the fact, to twist the truth to suit their purposes, as was often the case.

"The icing on the cake of that adventure is even worse. Joe Smith sent a lawyer back up there to Lee County to file suit against me and that Hancock County constable, charging us with illegal imprisonment and abuse. The court found in his favor and awarded him forty dollars in damages."

This time, Pogue could not stifle a laugh. "Did he get the money?"

"Not from me, he didn't. Not a penny. I wouldn't pay it. Illinois will have to come arrest me and try to get me extradited if they want that money, and then I'd tell them to leave me alone and not pay anyway."

Shooting pains in his leg told Pogue he had been sitting in one place long enough. He gathered the papers into one stack and put them back into the briefcase. "Can I keep these for a while? Go through the rest of them to see if there's anything that looks helpful, and ask you about it?" Reynolds agreed, so Pogue thought to push his luck.

"Would you mind, sir, driving out to the old Boggs place? I'd like to see it after dark and would surely appreciate your being there."

Reynolds mopped his brow and pulled a pocket watch as big around as a coffee saucer from his vest. "I reckon so. It ain't past my bedtime just yet."

———————————◆———————————

Spring Street was dark. Being out of the way as it was, and a dead-end to boot, it probably always was and always had been. Pogue stopped the rented buggy in front of the house, stepped down awkwardly, and wrapped a tie line around a hitching post. His passenger, meanwhile, maneuvered his bulk out of the carriage. The homeowner Pogue had talked to before answered his knock at the door and gave permission to the investigators to snoop around the yard.

Pogue fetched a lantern from the buggy but did not light it, wanting first to see, as much as possible, what the assailant had seen the night of May 6, 1842.

"Lot darker around here that night," Reynolds said. "'Bout nine o'clock, it was. Raining pitchforks and baby pigs. But right here is where we figured the shot was fired from. Blasted out this here window glass," he said, leaning forward and tapping lightly on a pane. "Boggs, he was sitting just a ways over from where that chair sits now, and a mite farther out in the room. No more than four feet from here.

"Pieces of his head, the inside and outside of it both, sprayed thataway," he said, pointing across the room. "Meat and bone, blood and brains, scalp and skin splattered everywhere. Lilburn sat there in that chair and squirted and seeped and dripped blood like a poleaxed molasses keg. And the balls that missed—thirteen of them, we counted—hit that wall over there."

"The girl and the baby?"

"Lucky, those two. They were on the floor about there," he pointed, "out of the line of sight and, thank goodness, low down enough that the only thing that hit them was bits and pieces of their daddy."

The Pinkerton man looked around, stepping here and there, pausing and circling around to see all directions. He bent at the waist to look through the window at a different angle. Finally, he lit the lantern.

"As I understand it, William Boggs ran to town for help."

"Yep. Billy hotfooted it to my office, and the deputy on duty rousted me out of my easy chair, and we come on out here."

"Did you notice anything unusual?"

Reynolds laughed and swiped at his forehead with a limp hanky. "Unusual? Unless you think two hundred of Independence, Missouri's finest citizens tramping around in the mud is unusual, I'd have to say no.

"Any hope there ever was of finding any footprints or a trail or clues of any kind was stomped out long before I got here. One of them fellows, though, he did find the pistol."

"Where was that?"

He waved his hanky at a spot just a few feet from the window and said, "Right about here. In a puddle. Lucky to have seen it, he was."

"You would think the shooter would have taken it with him. Or at least thrown it somewhere out of the way," Pogue said.

"You would. Here's the way I figured it—that pistol was a heavy piece of iron to begin with, and loaded for bear. My guess is, it bucked so bad when all that powder took fire that it jumped right out of his hand."

"That could explain why there was only one shot, too, I guess."

"Seems likely. It never made sense that a man set on killing Lilburn wouldn't have pumped more lead into him. But I don't guess we'll ever know."

Pogue wrote in his notebook for a few minutes and then asked about the gun. He learned it was a German-built, four-barrel pepperbox pistol. Something of a curiosity by now, the pepperbox style was common in an earlier time. This gun had been a square arrangement of four muzzle-loading barrels, each with its own nipple and cap. The barrels could be rotated after a shot to place a new barrel under the hammer.

"Like I said, it was a heavy gun to begin with. Most folks load a measure of powder and a single ball in each barrel. When I emptied the unfired barrels of that pistol, it was loaded about double what it should have been. The powder, I mean. Instead of a ball, that shooter had tamped down a heavy load of large-size buckshot—double-ought—fifteen or twenty balls to the barrel. It was plain he meant to tear up what he shot at. That being Lilburn Boggs, of course."

"It's getting late, Mr. Reynolds. I have taken up too much of your time today. But there is still much I would like to ask you. Can I see you again tomorrow?"

"Meet me for lunch."

Although his guts lurched at the idea, Pogue agreed.

———◆———

After a couple of days in jail in St. Louis, that bounty hunter shackled me hand and foot and loaded me in the dead of night onto a stagecoach to Independence. Terrible trip, that was. The driver ran us off the road and into a tree and upset the coach. It couldn't go on, for it was fallin' to pieces.

I could see right off that the crash had sheared the kingpin. Any fool could've seen it—'cept for that fool driver, he was so drunk. So we righted the coach, and I crawled around in the dirt and the dark and fixed the thing.

That whiskey-soaked driver wrecked us again not long after!

Told that bounty hunter I'd drive the infernal thing if they'd relieve me of them irons, but it was no go. But them other passengers talked him into it, them not wantin' to spend the night on the road waitin' for help. These bein' the same passengers, you understand, who used the cover of dark to abuse me with pokes and jabs and insults all along that road. But they's wantin' my help now, with mouths full of honey.

My keeper wouldn't unshackle me, but he boosted me up onto the driver's seat and kept me covered the whole way to the next station. While we waited for a company driver to replace that drunken fool we'd had, I was tossed into the jail in Jefferson City as compensation for my duty as a stage driver. Then we went on to Independence.

And so there I was. Right back where Boggs wanted me.

TWENTY

AFTER RELAXING FOR a couple of hours with a bottle of whiskey for a companion in a saloon downstairs at the hotel, Pogue spent the rest of the night sitting on the bed in his room, leaning back against the headboard. He sifted through the papers Reynolds had collected in the old leather valise, pausing from time to time to massage liniment into his smarting knee. Most of the papers were irrelevant. Those he stuffed back into the case, and he stacked those of interest on a small lamp table next to the bed.

Dawn was breaking when he finished the job, the outlines of the buildings on the street defining themselves in the growing light as he leaned on the sill to look out the window. He poured some water from the pitcher into the washbasin and gave his face a vigorous scrub, then folded his trousers neatly on the dresser, hung his shirt from a wall hook, and climbed into the bed for a few hours of sleep before meeting Reynolds for lunch. By then, perhaps he'd be hungry enough to face that café again.

◆

While they awaited delivery of the food they had ordered, Pogue slid a brittle, yellowed newspaper clipping across the table to Reynolds.

$300 REWARD
A PROCLAMATION
By the Governor of the State of Missouri.
Executive Department, City of Jefferson

WHEREAS, it has been represented to me, that the lion, LILBURN W. BOGGS, (late Governor of this State) on the evening of Friday the 6th instant, at his residence in the town of Independence, in the county of Jackson, was shot, (supposed mortally,) by some person or persons unknown, who is now at large.

NOW THEREFORE, I, THOMAS REYNOLDS, Governor of the State of Missouri, do offer a reward of Three Hundred Dollars, for the apprehension and delivery to the sheriff of Jackson County aforesaid, of the person guilty of the crime above mentioned.

Farther down the same column was:

Five Hundred Dollars Reward.
STOP THE MURDERER!!

The undersigned committee appointed by the citizens of Jackson County, Mo., to ferret out the assassin of Gov. Lilburn W. Boggs, offer a reward of $200, for the apprehension and delivery to our County Jail, of a man of the following description, and $300 in addition if he should be convicted.

A spare, well built man, about 5 feet 8 inches high, thin visage, pale complexion, regular features, keen, black eye, and a remarkably long, slender hand; had on when last seen, a half worn brown or grey beaverteen frock coat, a warm cloth vest, boots considerably worn, and dark drab, smooth cast broad brim hat. He landed at Owen's landing, Jackson County, off the steam boat Rowena, on the 27th day of April, and departed on the same boat, on the 29th of the same month, for Lexington Mo., and on the evening of the assassination was seen in the vicinity of Independence—which with many other corroborating circumstances, leaves no doubt of his guilt.—When first in Independence he called himself Tompkins, and professed to be a silver-smith by occupation, He is quite talkative, and has the appearance of an eastern man. He is about 38 or 40 years of age.

> *Independence, May 9, 1842.*
> *SAMUEL D. LUCAS,*
> *S. H. WOODSON,*
> *WILSON ROBERTS,*
> *JOHN KING,*
> *LEWIS JONES,*
> *Committee.*

Reynolds studied the clipping for a moment and then Pogue said, "That first bit is straightforward enough. Tell me about that second item."

"What?"

"Well, this man Tompkins. I've not heard the name nor heard of him before."

"Ain't nothing there. Wasn't then, isn't now."

"But these people—this committee—they seemed to think so. Says in that newspaper there was 'no doubt of his guilt.'"

"Mr. Pogue, for someone who claims to be a professional investigator, you can't tell well water in a teacup from wastewater in a thunder mug."

Reynolds smiled at the shock and surprise on the detective's face.

"You don't see my name on that list of that committee, do you? That so-called citizens committee wasn't nothing more than an attempt by a bunch of hotheaded vigilante-types to usurp my authority and take the law into their own hands. Fools, is what they was. Some of them were important men around town in them days, and I believe their 'committee' was nothing more than a barefaced attempt to curry public favor.

"That Tompkins fellow had nothing to do with anything.

Not that many folks could even remember his being around. If ever there was any 'corroborating circumstances' or whatever they called it, they never bothered to bring it to my attention or to anyone else in a position to do anything about it. Nothing but a lot of hot air," he said as he mopped his forehead.

Just then the dinner plates started landing on the table. Pogue's chicken looked marginally better than last night's meatloaf. The lima beans and fried potatoes beside it appeared suspect, however. But a glance across the table at the steaming, slippery-looking heap of corned beef and cabbage Reynolds had ordered convinced him the chicken was the better choice.

Pogue made no attempt at further conversation, picking at his dinner and watching Reynolds attack his with ferocity. After some time, a perceptible slowing occurred in the rate the man consumed the comestibles, so the detective took it as an opportunity to continue his inquiries.

———————◆———————

Somehow word had got out that we was comin'. Soon as that sheriff in Independence—Reynolds was his name—dragged me out of that coach, there was a sizeable mob yappin' and snappin' at me like a pack of rabid curs. They was wavin' ropes around, wantin' to string me up so as to save the citizens of Jackson County the cost of a trial. Them Missouri pukes could pay through the nose, far as I was concerned.

But Reynolds got me into the jail without much trouble. Them mobbers wasn't but a lot of talk. But when that sheriff dragged me before a judge some days later, they was there again, pokin' at me with clubs and kickin' at me—they's even teachin' their youngsters how to be brave, eggin' 'em on to abuse me same's they did. Thing was, the only reason they's so brave was I was in chains.

Still and all, dodgin' blows from them cowardly pukes was better than festerin' in that Jackson County jail. But that's where that judge said I was goin' to stay, without no chance of bail. Which made no never mind anyhow, on account of I didn't know of nobody with the means to go no bail had there been any.

Even though it was comin' on spring, that place was colder than cold. I never thought I'd ever get warm. Daytimes wasn't so bad. They let me sit in a cell upstairs. Now and then there'd be others locked up, and from time to time there'd be old newspapers they might read out to me.

At night, they chained me up in a pen in the cellar, without even a blanket. All there was to do was burrow into a pile of urine-soaked straw. Don't know if it got that way from other prisoners that had been locked up there, or if it came that way from the barnyard animals who'd bedded down in it before them. It was moldy, smelled awful, and was crawlin' with all manner of bugs.

As for food, there was little of it. Mostly table scraps hardly fit for the slop bucket. That and corn dodgers so hard you could knock down an ox with 'em. Which wouldn't have been a bad idea, come to think of it, 'cause then you could eat the ox.

But there was a family nearby that felt bad for me for some reason, and they'd sometimes send over a little black girl they had with a bucket of food. Once she came with an old whip handle she'd been playin' with and a ball of string. She tossed 'em through the bars when she left, and what I did was build me a fishin' pole. Baited it with a corn dodger and dangled it out the window, anglin' for passin' pukes. Didn't catch any, but I got me a few nibbles. Some of them folks was downright insulted to see that nasty hunk of corn bread danglin' there at the end of my line. Others, though, they got a laugh out of it.

That was about the only thing funny about that jail, I'm here to tell you.

TWENTY-ONE

"SO," POGUE SAID, pushing his plate aside, "what course did your investigations follow while the committee had everyone on the hunt for this Tompkins?"

Reynolds shoveled in a few more forkfuls of slimy cabbage, dabbed a wet spot off his chin with the napkin stuffed in his collar, and swallowed before he said, "Pretty early on the next morning I heard that Phil Uhlinger recognized the pistol that was fished out of the mud puddle out at the Boggs place.

"Uhlinger kept a store in Independence. Said the weapon had been stolen about a week before. Said this fellow named Brown who worked training horses for a man named Ward outside of town had been looking it over. He recollected as there wasn't anyone in the store that afternoon save Brown and a couple of darkies. Naturally, that's who he suspected of stealing it—the darkies, that is—and so he buttonholed the owner of them slaves, but it didn't turn up in a search of their belongings. He intended to broach Brown on the subject but hadn't had occasion as yet."

So, Reynolds said, he had made occasion himself. A trip to the Ward place to locate Brown revealed that he had packed up his kit bag and left that morning, the morning after the shooting. The sheriff nosed around the riverboat landings and found he'd boarded a downstream river steamer. Without more to go on, attempting to track him seemed useless at the time, as the suspect could disembark at any number of stops down the river or stay aboard to St. Louis, from where he could disappear in any direction.

But he did not give up on Brown.

"I nosed around, talked to several people. Turns out some old-timers had recognized this Brown, and his name wasn't Brown at all. It was Orrin Porter Rockwell. He'd lived in these parts back in '33 or thereabouts. Him and his father ran a ferry up on the Big Blue. Married a girl who lived there. Seems that when the Mormons got run out of here back then, the Rockwells quit the country, but the girl's folks didn't. They're still here. Found his wife there, back then, with a newborn babe in arms. Says she came back to her folks' place to have the baby but claimed her man was in Nauvoo and had been all along. But enough people who knew him knew otherwise."

Inquiries to the northern counties where the Mormons experienced their later troubles in Missouri returned more information about this man.

"Rockwell was a well-known thug in the Mormon wars up there in '38 and '39. They say he was a captain of the Danites, a night-riding Mormon mob that spread terror all across that country. Burned places, killed and stole stock, destroyed crops, pistol whipped and roughed up anyone who argued—and some just for sport. Even killed some folks, they say.

"Later, when Joe Smith and some others were in jail in Liberty, awaiting trial for treason and murder, Rockwell smuggled them tools that nearly allowed them to escape."

It didn't take long for suspicion concerning Rockwell to spread, and he was located among the Mormons in Nauvoo. Belief in Rockwell's guilt grew when the apostate saint John Bennett wrote to Boggs claiming he had evidence that Rockwell had shot him on orders from Joseph Smith. The ex-governor swore out the affidavit that led to repeated attempts to have the accused men arrested in Illinois and returned to Missouri for trial. Rockwell and Smith were arrested and jailed in Nauvoo but soon released.

"After that, Rockwell flew the coop. Didn't see or hear hide nor hair of him for more than six months," Reynolds said. "Joe Smith, he got arrested a couple more times—once by me, like I told you. But he proved too slippery, and we never could get him here for trial."

That prompted Pogue to retrieve the next piece of paper he had extracted from the pile to ask about. It was a copy of a receipt, over Reynolds's signature, dated March 11, 1843. Made out to Messrs. Parker and Fox, it acknowledged delivery of Orrin Porter Rockwell to the sheriff of Jackson County.

"I remember that day," Reynolds said. "Them lowlife bounty hunters had snagged Rockwell getting off a boat in St. Louis. Probably on his way back to Nauvoo. Just luck, was all it was. They happened to be hanging around on the wharf when he walked down the gangplank of a riverboat.

"They hauled Rockwell here to Independence and wouldn't give him up until I wrote that out for them so they could claim the reward. That delay nearly caused a riot."

"How so?" Pogue asked, pushing an empty chair away from the table, grabbing his stiff knee with both hands, and lifting the leg up onto the seat.

"Word had spread that Rockwell was at the jail, and a sizeable crowd—more like a mob, I guess—gathered. They were yelling and carrying on, wanting to string Rockwell up then and there and save the county the cost of a trial. I managed to hold them off and got Rockwell inside and locked up."

Reynolds swiped at his face with his handkerchief and laughed. "Only funny thing about that situation was that I tried to take the wrong man. There was this other fellow who got off the coach, you see, and I looked him over and asked one of them bounty hunters if he had given them any trouble. 'That ain't Rockwell,' he said, 'this here's your man!' I swear to this day that other fellow looked guilty!"

That was not the only time he had saved Rockwell from a lynching, Reynolds said. He'd been kept in a cell on the second floor of the jailhouse, and in April a cell mate was locked in with him. Reynolds said the jailer had neglected to relieve the new prisoner of his belongings. Rockwell pawed through the man's saddlebags and found some fire steels, which he used to file through the chain on his legs. Meanwhile, his fellow prisoner slipped a slave girl some money when she brought them a meal, and with her next delivery she included a knife.

Later, when the jailer unlocked the cell to gather the dinnerware, the prisoners shoved past and locked him in the cell. They ran down the stairs and out the back door, and headed for an alley. Rockwell scrambled over a high fence and took off—but came back to help the other man over the fence. The delay was just long enough for the alarm to spread and both men were soon back in custody.

Reynolds said, "When we got Rockwell back to the jail, there was a lynch mob milling around. These men were angry, and they'd have overrun us and strung up Rockwell to a tree limb if we hadn't acted fast. They even had the rope ready. But I hollered out that there wouldn't be any hanging done that night. I ordered my deputies to shoot if necessary, and the holes in the ends of them muzzles staring at them mobbers stopped them long enough for us to get that jailbreaking Mormon back inside.

"No cell for him this time. I hauled him down to the dungeon in the cellar and chained him hand and foot. I'd see to it he didn't slip out of there again—not that he didn't try. After a while I unhobbled him so's he could stretch out to sleep. But that snaky fellow pulled a stovepipe out of the ceiling and slithered through a hole that wasn't much more than a foot square.

"Lucky for us, it opened into a locked room. We found him sleeping in there one morning—he'd picked the lock with the bail from a water bucket that was in the room, but apparently the half-starved fool was too tired to keep on."

"Half-starved?"

"That's right. We had him on short rations, which is about half of what was not much to begin with. But he sure deserved punishment. No one ever said the Jackson County jail was supposed to be a fancy hotel—or even a low-rent boarding house, for that matter. He was there because he was a criminal, not a welcome guest. I'll not apologize for his treatment—or that of any other prisoner I kept during my term."

Pogue shuffled through his stack of papers as Reynolds shoved a few more forkfuls of greasy cabbage into his mouth. The way he flung the fork around, Pogue hoped he didn't stab himself.

———◆———

I spent nine months in that Missouri jail. After a time, I quit wonderin' when I'd ever get my day in court. Just goes to show how Boggs still had his finger in things, even with him not bein' governor nor nothin' else anymore. He believed I'd shot him, and that was enough for him and the rest of them Missouri pukes to lock me up and forget about me.

After I's there a couple of months, another man, name of Watson, got himself tossed into the jail for forgery or some such. He landed in my cell one day, baggage and all. We talked some, and I asked what he had in them saddlebags. He tossed them my way sayin' to have at 'em, but said he thought it unlikely I'd find anything useful.

I's surprised to find some flint and steel in there. Ol' Watson, he couldn't see why I was so happy about it, nor could he feature what I was up to when I took to sawin' on my leg irons with one of them fire starters. He caught on, finally. And while I worked at my shackles, I told him how I figured we could get out of there.

Took me two days to part them cuffs. In the meantime, we'd paid that little black girl who carried me food with some money Watson had—he might've printed it up hisself, for all I know—and she hid a knife in some victuals.

Jailer come by in the evenin' to gather our slops and supper dishes, and when he unlocked the door I jumped up and heaved him into the corner and scampered out of there and locked him in that cage. We headed down the stairs, and that jailer's wife was comin' up. Scared her near to death, we did, but we just shoved her aside and kept on goin' out the back door.

I made my way over this high fence and into the alley and was on my way when Watson hollered he couldn't get over. Like a fool, I went back. Climbed back up on that fence, I did, and hauled him over by his shirt collar.

By then, that hollerin' jailer and his wife had folks already lookin' for us, and we was caught 'fore we got far.

Reynolds, that sheriff, was so mad about the whole situation—and a mite red in the face—that instead of takin' me back to the jail, he shoved me into that mob of bloodthirsty pukes, tellin' 'em to do with me what they wanted. "Get a rope," somebody hollered, and they took to layin' hands on me.

That woke Reynolds up, I guess, and he shouted 'em down and took me back to that jail after all, with them mobbers fightin' to get ahold of me all the way into the jail and right up until the sheriff slammed the cell door. Deputies had to draw down on that mob 'fore they'd let up.

After that, he kept me chained up crosswise, wrists to the off ankles, so's I couldn't even stand up straight. Them wrist cuffs was real tight, I'll tell you. But they starved me down so bad from then on, I could soon enough slide 'em up past my elbows.

I'd been free for a bit. But now there I was, back in Boggs's clutches.

TWENTY-TWO

THE FURY SOON SUBSIDED—or was buried under a smothering layer of food—and Reynolds pushed his plate away, swabbed a hanky across the shine of his forehead, and asked, "What else you got there?"

Pogue handed him the scrawled draft of a letter.

Jackson County Jail, Independence, Mo.

Joseph Smith, Sir,

At the request of Orrin Porter Rockwell, who is now confined in our jail, I write you a few lines concerning his affairs. He is held to bail in the sum of $5,000, and wishes some of his friends to bail him out. He also wishes some friend to bring his clothes to him. He is in good health and pretty good spirits. My own opinion is, after conversing with several persons here, that it would not be safe for any of Mr. Rockwell's friends to come here, notwithstanding I have written the above at his request; neither do I think bail would be taken (unless it was some responsible person well known here as a resident of this state). Any letter to Mr. Rockwell, (post paid,) with authority expressed on the back for me to open it, will be handed to him without delay. In *the meantime he will be humanely treated and dealt with kindly until discharged by due course of law.*

Yours, etc.
s/J. H. Reynolds
Sheriff, Jackson County, Mo.

"Yeah, I remember writing that. I'll tell you this—I didn't enjoy having to play secretary for that back-shooting scoundrel. But he was illiterate as an oaktree stump. Couldn't read a word nor write more than an X for his mark."

Pogue made a note before asking, "You said in the letter it would be unsafe for his friends to visit him. Did anyone risk it?"

"No. He hadn't but one visitor the whole time he was locked up, and that was months later, after we brought him back from Liberty. His mother showed up and boohooed over him for a while. They huddled in the corner and exchanged who-knows-what infernal secrets. Seemed his Mormon 'friends' didn't give a hoot about him.

"I did offer one time to take him to see his friend Joe Smith—on conditions—but he refused."

"Conditions?"

"The deal was, he'd arrange a meeting out in the open somewhere—somewhere out on the prairie away from all his henchmen. Then, the plan was, we'd lay hold on Joe Smith and turn Rockwell loose. Even offered him any amount of money he named, to boot."

"Apparently he did not accept the trade."

"No. Said he'd see me damned first. Told him he could rot in jail and we'd get Smith without his help. And we tried. We certainly tried. He was in custody three or four times. Either his own courts in Nauvoo turned him loose or the state of Illinois wouldn't let us have him."

"Backing up a minute—what had Rockwell been charged with? If bail was set, there must have been a court appearance. Who was his lawyer?"

"Soon after we jailed him, a couple of sharpers came by offering to represent him. They convinced Rockwell to sign over his property to them for safekeeping—said I couldn't be trusted with it. They took his watch and a brace of pistols and a nasty-looking Bowie knife, and Rockwell never saw them nor his stuff ever again.

"The Justice of the Peace set bail. There was a grand jury convened, but they refused to indict. I wasn't privy to the proceedings, so I don't know exactly what got into those idiot jurors. Claimed there wasn't enough evidence for a true bill. And somehow—don't know how, they wouldn't say—Rockwell convinced them he was miles away from Independence when Boggs was shot. All balderdash, if you ask me."

"But you didn't free Rockwell when he wasn't indicted?"

"No! Like I told you, there was a lot of politics mixed up in this whole affair. I was told to keep him in custody until they could figure out something or some way to convict him. I didn't want to turn the guilty fool loose anyway.

"Later in the summer, along about August it seems, Rockwell was hauled into court. Circuit Judge name of Ryland told him the grand jury hadn't indicted him in the Boggs affair. Rockwell howled and hurrahed, but his good humor didn't last long. Judge said he had been indicted for breaking jail. Asked him if he had a lawyer, and Rockwell said no and that he couldn't afford one. Judge told him to look around the courtroom and choose one.

"Well, Rockwell recognized Alexander Doniphan. He'd helped the Mormons before. Fact is, he saved Joe Smith from being put before a militia firing squad up at Far West. Should have let them shoot him, if you ask me. Anyway, Doniphan complained and carried on about how he didn't have the time but Judge Ryland told him to shut up and get to work."

The lawyer's first move, Reynolds said, was to seek a change of venue, as he did not believe Rockwell could get a fair trial in Jackson County. The judge agreed and sent the case to Clay County, where Doniphan lived. Deputies were sent to transfer the prisoner to the jail in Liberty. A vigilante group out of Independence attempted to overtake them on the road, and the lawmen and outlaw had to ride for their lives.

Rockwell cooled his heels for ten days in the Liberty Jail before being sent back to Independence. The judge, finding some technical irregularity in the change-of-venue order, denied a hearing and sent the whole distasteful mess back to Jackson County. Again, the party escaped an attempt to murder the prisoner during transfer, this time by taking a different road at the last minute to avoid the mob.

Weeks later, court convened in Jackson County under Judge Austin King, who had a decided distaste for Mormons. He accepted Rockwell's plea of not guilty of jailbreak and seated a jury.

Doniphan's arguments for his client followed two lines. First, the law on Missouri's books said breaking out of jail was a matter of breaking through a wall or door, or picking or breaking a lock— none of which Rockwell had done. The judge, however, wasn't buying it and ruled that forcing his way out of the door when the jailer opened it satisfied the law's requirements—no matter what the book said.

The lawyer's other line of reasoning was that his client had been improperly held—since Rockwell had not been indicted by the grand jury or otherwise charged with a crime, he should not have been in the Jackson County Jail. Therefore, he argued, Rockwell could not possibly be guilty of breaking out of a jail where he should not have been in the first place.

"The jury must have swallowed one or the other lines that shyster Doniphan fed them," Reynolds said. "They came back with a guilty verdict, but ruled the punishment for the offense was five minutes in the county jail."

"So he walked," Pogue said.

"Yes, but it wasn't in no five minutes. More like five hours. We weren't too happy with the sentence, so I kept Rockwell locked up while me and Judge King tried to cook up some other charges to hold him on. But Doniphan kept after us like a hound dog after a bitch in heat, and we finally had to let that murdering blackguard go.

"Only good thing about the whole deal was that I never again had to lay eyes on that back-shooter. I'll tell you, I was sick and tired of Porter Rockwell by then. Still would have liked to hang the fool, though."

Pogue made himself a note to look up Alexander Doniphan.

———————◆———————

Rottin' in that Independence jail like to've turned me into an animal. Leastways I come to look like one. My hair and whiskers grew long. And, of course, not bein' given the luxury of a bath, them long locks was greasy and tangled.

Got to the point where the vermin and varmints in that jail couldn't tell me apart from my stinkin' straw bed. They's crawlin' all over me all the time, makin' a meal of whatever nasty ooze there was to be had. Leastways they was eatin'—me, I got next to nothin' to eat, and what did come through the bars wasn't worth the time it took to chew it. But I learned soon enough what I didn't eat of a Tuesday came back on the same plate on Wednesday.

See, that Sheriff Reynolds was so aggravated at me for fleein' his jail that he never cared a whit afterward if I lived or died. He's as soon I did die, seemed like to me.

Still and all, they'd have rather had Joseph than me. Boggs tried every wily way he could conjure up to get him in his clutches. Even tried to get me in on one of his schemes. Leastways I'm bettin' it was Boggs.

See, Reynolds kept after me for days to get Joseph to come to Missouri to fetch me out of jail. Said if I could get just him inside the borders of the state, or anywheres else out of the way, he'd not only turn me loose, he'd pay me a reward. Told me I could name my price, and him and them pukes would raise it, whatever it was. Told him I'd see all of them damned first. Told me, that bein' the case, I could rot in that dungeon.

My treatment didn't get any better after that, I'm here to tell you.

One time Reynolds went to Illinois with a handful of Boggs's trumped-up paperwork to get Joseph arrested so's he could haul him back to Missouri. I don't rightly know what happened, but that sheriff came back empty-handed and mad as anything.

After that, things was worse still. Bad as that lawdog hated me and every other Mormon, his ill feelin's weren't nothin' compared to Boggs's.

And on account of Reynolds was mostly just packin' Boggs's water in this whole affair, his failin' to get Joseph likely had ol' Boggs on him like them vermin was on me.

TWENTY-THREE

ALEXANDER DONIPHAN was not hard to find. Pogue's inquiries soon revealed he was still practicing law across the Missouri River in Ray County, some fifty miles away in the city of Richmond. The Pinkerton man wrote, requesting an appointment.

While awaiting a reply, he made something of a nuisance of himself at the Jackson County courthouse, combing through dusty boxes of records, seeking any documents related to the Boggs shooting, the proceedings of the grand jury that failed to indict Rockwell, his trial or hearings, legal opinions from judges, anything—anything—that would give him a better grasp of what happened those years ago.

He found nothing.

He did, however, find something to his liking in a dry goods store he passed repeatedly on his trips between the hotel and the courthouse.

Independence, Mo.

Emily Elizabeth, My Dear,
Every day that passes I think of you and miss you. When I at last see you again, it will be difficult for anyone to force me from your presence. I trust you are doing well and hope you are a delight to your mother and are not causing her any grief.

Here with this note is another occupant for your stables. But this one, as you will see by its big ears, is not a horse. It is a sort of cousin to the horse that is common here in Missouri where I have been working for a time. It is called a mule—its mother is a mare, and its father, called Jack, is a donkey.

I hope you enjoy your Missouri Mule. Pull the string and see what happens!

All my love until I can hug you again,
Father

The toy wooden mule wrapped in the package stood four inches high, including the wood block it stood on. Only its front hooves were on the ground, the hind legs kicking outward. Out of a hole in the block came a short string with a small wooden ball on the end. Give it a tug and the mule's hind legs kicked higher while its head and neck tipped downward. Then, by some hidden mechanism, both ends automatically sprung back to where they started.

Pogue's childish fascination with the kicking mule made him confident it would keep Emily Elizabeth occupied for many happy hours in his absence.

And, he hoped, remind the girl she did, indeed, have a father.

———◆———

The man rose from his desk and, it seemed to Pogue, kept rising and rising. To say that Alexander Doniphan cut an imposing figure would be a gross understatement. He stood, the detective surmised, nearly six-and-a-half feet tall. Broad shouldered, well proportioned, and with a face that begged to be cast in bronze, he looked every bit the military man he had been.

In looking into the background of the man he would be meeting, Pogue learned that Doniphan had served as a brigadier general in the Missouri state militia during the Mormon wars, and a colonel of the Missouri Mounted Volunteers in Stephen W. Kearny's army during the Mexican War. When Civil War threatened, he was offered a commission as colonel in the Missouri State Guard and the rank of general in the Union Army—both of which he refused, choosing instead to sit out the conflict owing to mixed loyalties.

"Alexander Doniphan, at your service," he said with an extended hand.

"I am pleased you agreed to see me, sir."

"Looking into the Boggs affair, you said. Sorry business, that. But why dredge it up all these years later?"

"At the request of the Boggs family, sir. William Boggs engaged the Pinkerton Detective Agency and, as I was in California at the time wrapping up other agency business, the assignment came to me."

"But why? What do they hope to accomplish at this late date?"

"Peace of mind, I suppose. Some sense of satisfaction. It seems they—Bill, at least—can't put it to rest without a resolution of some kind."

"That certainly was a traumatic time for the boy. Seeing his father shot up like that in their own home," Doniphan said, shaking his head and looking sorrowful. "Sit."

The lawyer offered a drink, which Pogue declined.

"Have you gotten a handle on the affair?" Doniphan asked.

"Hard to say. Lots of finger pointing, but not much in the way of hard evidence to go on."

"Yes, yes. That's much the way it was at the time. No witnesses. No damning evidence. No convincing proof of any kind against anyone. Sad business, that. So, how can I help you?"

Pogue unfolded his notebook, turned to a fresh page, dragged the pencil across his tongue, and said, "Porter Rockwell was accused of the crime. You represented him in court. I wonder if you'd tell me how that came to be."

Doniphan launched into a lengthy tale that began in 1833, when the Mormons were run out of Jackson County. He represented several of them in defending their right to live in peace in the county and later in filing claims to recover property appropriated by the old settlers who forced the Saints from their homes. Then, while serving in the state legislature, he helped create Caldwell County in the unsettled region to the north as a homeland for the homeless Mormons.

When trouble found them there, the militia officer found himself on the other side of the fight, leading troops against his former clients in the Mormon War of 1838. Doniphan said the causes of conflict were many, but laid most of the blame on the Mormons for not confining themselves to Caldwell County. As they spilled over into adjacent counties, trouble started with settlers there.

Doniphan's Clay County militia unit was among several called up by Governor Boggs and sent to restore order. In the midst of much raiding and burning and bloody fighting between Mormons and Missourians, one of Doniphan's counterparts, General John Clark, was issued an unprecedented order over the signature of Governor Boggs. Doniphan located a copy in a file drawer and passed it across the desk to Pogue.

> Sir—Since the order of this morning to you, directing you to cause four hundred mounted men to be raised within your division, I have received by Amos Rees, Esq. of Ray county and Wiley C. Williams, Esq., one of my aides, information of the most appalling character, which entirely changes the face of things, and places the Mormons in the attitude of an open and avowed defiance of the laws, and of having made war upon the people of this State.

> Your orders are, therefore, to hasten your operations with all possible speed. The Mormons must be treated as enemies, and must be exterminated or driven from the State if necessary, for the public peace—their outrages are beyond all description. If you can increase your force, you are authorized to do so to any extent you may consider necessary.

> I have just issued orders to Maj. Gen. Willock of Marion county, to raise five hundred men, and to march them to the northern part of Daviess, and there unite with General

Doniphan, of Clay, who has been ordered with five hundred men to proceed to the same point for the purpose of intercepting the retreat of the Mormons to the north. They have been directed to communicate with you by express, you can also communicate with them if you find it necessary.

Instead, therefore, of proceeding as at first directed to reinstate the citizens in their homes, you will proceed immediately to Richmond and then operate against the Mormons.

Brig. Gen. Parks of Ray, has been ordered to have four hundred of his Brigade in readiness to join you at Richmond. The whole force will be placed under your command.

I am very respectfully,
your ob't serv't,
s/L. W. Boggs, Commander-in-Chief

Pogue read the orders through quickly, then returned to the middle of the document to reassure himself he had read what he thought, and that he had understood what he read. While it was no surprise—others had told him of it—the words on paper were still shocking.

" 'The Mormons must be treated as enemies, and must be exterminated or driven from the State,' " he read aloud to Doniphan. "So Governor Boggs essentially declared war on a group of his own citizens?"

"That he did."

Pogue read it again.

"I don't know the situation here at the time. But I cannot imagine it being so bad as to require such orders."

"Neither could I. But, then, remember that I already suffered from a reputation as a friend to the Mormons—which meant my opinion was neither sought nor listened to when offered. Which didn't matter much at the time, for nearly every other officer and soldier in every militia unit cheered at the governor's orders and were eager to enforce them—the extermination part of it, that is.

"The alternative of expelling them from the state was an odious proposition so far as they were concerned. The citizen militia of Missouri was ready and willing to wipe out the Mormons, and it was only through luck that such was avoided."

"And how was it avoided?"

Doniphan sketched out the essentials of the end times of the Mormon War in Missouri, 1838 and 1839. While the Mormon militia fortified their stronghold at Far West for a final, decisive battle, some 2,500 government troops converged on the place. The overwhelming show of force convinced Joseph Smith and other Mormon leaders to abandon any notion of armed conflict and seek terms.

"The head of the Mormon militia said Smith knew the terms and agreed to them. Others said he was sold down the river. Whatever the situation, when he came out to surrender he got more than he bargained for. He was arrested, along with a few others, and held hostage. Surrounded by hostile and threatening troops, they spent a long, cold night on the ground.

"A military court, as ill-advised and illegal as such a charade possibly could be, convened and sentenced Joseph Smith and half a dozen others to execution. Utter nonsense! Courts-martial, by their very nature, exist to enforce military regulations. No one of those men on trial was a member of the state militia or a part of any other government force. You simply cannot subject civilians to military justice!

"I and a few others argued for the Mormons. But another general—Sam Duncan, it was—held sway, and the men were sentenced to die by firing squad. Look at this—"

The lawyer handed Pogue another page from his files. It was from Duncan, addressed to Doniphan, and read:

> Sir: You will take Joseph Smith and the other prisoners into the public square of Far West and shoot them at 9 o'clock tomorrow morning.

Pogue looked up after reading the order, and Doniphan handed him another page; a draft copy of his reply to Duncan's orders:

It is cold-blooded murder. I will not obey your order. My brigade shall march for Liberty tomorrow at 8 o'clock and if you execute these men, I will hold you responsible before an earthly tribunal, so help me God.

"The rest doesn't matter," Doniphan said. "Smith and the others survived and were jailed in my town of Liberty for several months. The Mormons were driven off, their property appropriated and plundered. They spent a miserable few months slogging through the cold and snow and mud, making their way to Illinois. No one knew what to do with Joseph and the other prisoners, and finally, in the spring, they were allowed to escape and flee eastward to join their people.

"But I have wasted too much of your time on tangential issues. You are here to learn about Porter Rockwell and the shooting of Governor Boggs."

———◆———

'Long about August they finally dragged me back into court. That judge said the grand jury had not brought an indictment against me on account of a lack of evidence. I let out a whoop and holler, figurin' I'd be walkin' out of there any minute.

That judge put an end to that right off. He went on and said them jurors had turned in a true bill on me for bustin' out of jail! He asked how did I plead, and I said not guilty by a sight.

Well, that judge said I'd be needin' a lawyer, then, as there would be a trial comin'. That was the first time I'd heard mention of a lawyer for months. Fact is, I hadn't seen hide nor hair of no attorney all them months in that Independence jail. Which was fine by me, I suppose, on account of the last so-called lawyers I'd talked to hadn't done nothin' but fleece me.

See, it was back when I was bein' held in St. Louis right after that bounty hunter grabbed me gettin' off the riverboat. Couple of men came to the jail sayin' they was lawyers wantin' to represent me. Suggested I turn over my belongin's to 'em to hold, so's the law wouldn't take 'em once we got to Independence. So, I told that bounty hunter to give 'em what I had. They waltzed out of there with my pocket watch, a good Bowie knife, and a brace of pistols—and that's the last I seen of them two shysters or any of my stuff.

Anyways, the judge asked if I had the means to pay a lawyer, which of course I hadn't. By that time, I couldn't rightly claim the shirt on my back, it bein' nothin' but rags and tatters. So he said to have a look-see around the courtroom and take my pick of any of the attorneys that was there on other business.

Which I did. I saw Alexander Doniphan and remembered him from back in Far West. He was that militia officer who wouldn't put Joseph in front of a firin' squad and kept all them other officers from doin' so. I knowed he'd done some other legal work for some Mormons back in them days too, so I figured I wouldn't do no better than him.

They marched me back to jail even though the court said I didn't do what they locked me up for in the first place. They wasn't goin' to turn me loose no matter what. Only reason I could see for it was that Boggs wanted it that way.

TWENTY-FOUR

ALEXANDER DONIPHAN ROSE from behind the desk in his law office and walked to a window overlooking a quiet, tree-lined street. Sunlight and shadow dappled a face lost in thought. After a few minutes, during which the Pinkerton man caught up on his note-keeping and noted some questions to pose to the lawyer, Doniphan turned and again addressed his guest.

"I don't know as I ever laid eyes on Porter Rockwell until the day he pointed me out in the courtroom in Jackson County and the judge assigned me the man's defense," Doniphan said as he returned to the desk chair.

"Oh, it's possible he or his family were among the many, many Mormons whose stolen properties I attempted to recover after they were driven from the Independence area back in 1833 and 1834, but I do not recall any personal audience with the man. I heard his name, later, during the difficulties in the northern counties. He was among those associated with the Danites."

Pogue said, "I have read of and been told about them. The accounts vary. Mormons say they were simply a protection against mobbers. Others say they were murdering night riders."

Doniphan chuckled. "Sentiments typical of the time. I suspect those opinions have held firm through the intervening years, and I believe it will remain so for all history. Personally, I know little of their activities. They existed, no doubt. They spread terror, no doubt. But they, I believe, were little different from their counterparts among the old settlers of Missouri."

"How so?"

"Many men of my acquaintance, including some in my militia unit, were called up as sworn soldiers of the government. But, when not on duty, they rode with vigilante bands—the Mormons called them mobs—bullying the Mormons. Likewise, the Mormons organized militia units of their own, and many of those who served also rode at times with the Danites. The difference being, of course, that at least the Missouri militia had the force of law on its side; the Mormons had no such sanction.

"All their military activities were, in the strictest sense, illegal. I, and many others, believed the Mormons had been ill-used in many instances and their rights infringed upon, if not outright trampled. Legal or no, acts in self-defense are understandable, even justified. The Danites, however, from reports I heard, often crossed the line. There is no doubt they plundered and burned Gallatin and a couple of other communities and committed other nefarious deeds.

"Porter Rockwell was said to be in the thick of it, even an occasional leader of Danite bands."

Following the Mormon surrender, when Joseph Smith and other Mormon leaders were jailed in Liberty, Doniphan—who represented the Prophet—was aware of Rockwell's many visits to the jail as a messenger. The Danite was also accused in the attempted jailbreak—the prisoners all but broke through the walls using tools he smuggled in during his visits. But jailers discovered the near-breach, and Rockwell, fearing he would join his brethren behind bars, appeared no more at Liberty Jail.

"That's the last I heard of the man until the aforementioned day in court when he sought my representation. I was not pleased about his choice, I'll tell you that."

"Why?"

"As I told Judge Ryland at the time, my calendar was full. The last thing I needed was an indigent, unpopular client. Despite my reluctance, I determined to do my best for him, as that is a lawyer's duty. I said as much to my new client but suggested he not get his hopes up, given popular opinion against him."

Pogue made a note to himself, turned to a fresh page, and asked, "Did you share that opinion? Did you think him guilty?"

"Truth be told, I had not paid much attention to the particulars of the case. I had heard about it, of course. The shooting was in all the newspapers, and the subject of much conversation everywhere, including courthouse hallways. So, I had a general understanding of events, but I had formed no opinion of Mr. Rockwell's involvement in it one way or the other. As it turned out, the facts of the case—let alone my own opinion—did not enter into the situation."

"How so?"

"I was appointed Mr. Rockwell's counsel in August. He had, at that point, been jailed since March. No charges had been filed against him in all that time. No hearing had been held. He had not been afforded any opportunity to speak for himself in court, confront his accusers, or address the evidence against him. All that, of course, flies in the face of the rights every citizen is afforded under our laws and the Constitution of our country.

"The occasion of his appearance that day was to be informed by the court that the grand jury had refused to indict him for shooting Governor Boggs. In normal circumstances, the prisoner would have walked free. But Sheriff Reynolds and Judge Ryland had no intention of releasing Mr. Rockwell. They were determined to hold him regardless of legalities. They informed him that he had been indicted for escaping from jail and would be held and brought to trial on that charge."

Doniphan went on to describe his strategy.

"The first thing I did was move for a change of venue. It was obvious that the people of Jackson County were too inflamed against my client to judge him fairly on that or any other charge. I believed, as well, that Judge Ryland himself suffered such bias that he would manipulate events against my client. I sought and received reassignment of the case and was granted a change of venue to Clay County. Mr. Rockwell was transferred to Liberty under guard, and very nearly killed along the way.

"My strategy proved futile, however. The courts in Clay County wanted nothing to do with the case. The magistrate there delayed putting the case on the calendar and studied the change of venue order letter by letter, looking for some reason—any reason—to avoid taking action. Finally, he declared some technical deficiency in the preparation of the order and sent us back to Jackson County. And, again, Mr. Rockwell was in great danger on the return trip—he only just escaped certain death, thanks to a last-minute change of route.

"I tried for weeks—months—to get Mr. Rockwell into a courtroom, but Ryland's court was out of session, and my client rotted in jail. His mother visited a time or two and brought with her from Nauvoo the sum of one hundred dollars, sent by Joseph Smith as legal fees. I finally managed to get a special session of the court called, with Judge Austin King of Ray County presiding. If Judge Ryland was biased, Judge King was no improvement. He had lost a brother-in-law at the hands of the Mormons years before in Independence and hated everything about the Saints.

"And so he immediately dismissed my motion for a dismissal based on the fact that Mr. Rockwell had not actually broken out of jail according to the statute as he had broken no lock, broke through no wall, broken down no door, nor committed any other action or activity that met the requirements of the law."

"I must admit it sounds like a long shot," Pogue interjected. "Rockwell did escape and was at large."

"Indeed it was and indeed he did. But a defense attorney is obligated to make the government prove the charges according to the laws as written and on the books. Another day it might have worked. And the fact was—and is—that my client had been held all those months without charge, therefore, according to law, should not have been in jail in the first place. It stands to reason, then, that a man jailed illegally can hardly be called to account for leaving said jail."

"I understand, however, that the jury disagreed."

"In a manner of speaking. Given the judge's prejudicial

instructions they could hardly do otherwise. But, bless their souls, the jurors saw the absurdity of the prosecution's charges, and while they found Mr. Rockwell guilty, their sentence of no less than five minutes in the Jackson County jail revealed their true opinion."

Still, the lawyer told Pogue, the judge and the sheriff held his client overnight, rather than the five minutes the jury ordered, attempting to cook up other charges on which to hold Rockwell.

Pogue winced at the pain in his wounded knee on rising. He thanked Alexander Doniphan for his time and turned to leave but stopped at the office door to say, "Tell me, counselor. If it had been necessary to defend Rockwell against charges of shooting Boggs, what do you think the outcome would have been?"

Doniphan did not even take a moment to consider the question.

"We would have won going away, despite all the prosecution would have done, no doubt, to stack the desk against us. The evidence just wasn't there. When the grand jury, with less stringent rules of evidence and no defense by the accused, refused to indict, despite the political pressure applied against them, you can rest assured there was no case to be made against Mr. Rockwell."

"One last question, if I may—did you ever ask Rockwell if he did it?"

"No, sir. Such knowledge is of little importance to a defense attorney," Doniphan said. "And, the fact is, I did not want to know.

———————◆———————

That lawyer Alexander Doniphan convinced the judge to move my trial somewhere else, where folks didn't hate Mormons so much. Clay county was where they decided to do it, which meant I'd be locked up in that Liberty Jail where Joseph and them was held for so long.

A couple of deputies was assigned to move me up there, and they tied me onto the back of a rough-gaited old nag not fit to ride. Not only was my feet roped together under the horse's belly, my hands was tied behind my back.

We hustled on to the river before folks was aware I was out where they could get at me. Leastways that's what we thought. We got to the ferry just as it was pullin' up to the landing on yonder side, and I see'd a passel of men get off and disappear into the woods. Looked mighty suspicious to me. Them deputies asked that ferryman about it. Never mind, he said, they was just some woodcutters. Don't know how they would've cut a tree, them bein' empty-handed and all. No ax, saw, maul, nor any tool among 'em. That, and they all had saddle horses rather than work teams. Anyhow, even them lawdogs figured it was trouble.

So we kept our eyes and ears open along that road through them woods. We was a couple, three miles along the road when of a sudden we heard 'em crashin' through the underbrush in them woods. Couldn't be certain, on account of we couldn't see nothin', but with all that ruckus, it had to have been them, and they had to have been comin' for us.

One of them deputies larruped my horse on the rump with his bridle reins, and they spurred up their mounts, and we went tearin' down that road. Without no hands and with my feet hobbled it was all I could do to stay aboard. But we rode it out and made it safe to Liberty.

That trip turned out to be a fool's errand. The judge up there in Clay County said the paperwork wasn't in order, so after coolin' my heels in Liberty Jail for a week or two, they sent me back to Independence.

Jail there weren't no different than before—they kept my legs shackled and fed me on slops, as always. My old mother showed up there to see me sometime in October. She'd been worried sick about me, but seein' me locked up in that dungeon and chained up like some circus animal like to've killed the poor woman. I don't think she even stayed overnight in that town but beat it back to Nauvoo. Said she was goin' to pester Joseph till he figured some way to get me out of there. He harangued the Saints to cough up what money they could, and my mother came back with a hundred dollars to pay Alexander Doniphan for my defense.

I weren't in no mood to wait. I'd gaunted up so much by then that I could slip right out of them wrist and ankle cuffs. There was an old stove in that cellar that never held a fire in all my time there, and I managed to work the chimney pipe loose. That opened up a hole in the ceiling, couldn't have been much more'n a foot across, but I managed to scrape my way up through it, barkin' off a goodly bit of my hide doin' it.

But all that got me was into a cell upstairs, and the door to that bein' locked up tight. There was a honey bucket there with a wire bail, which I twisted off and used for to pick that lock. But I had no luck, so dropped back down through that hole before mornin' thinkin' to try again the next night.

My luck weren't no better. Matter of fact, it was worse. I wore myself out so bad squeezin' through that hole and workin' on that lock that I dropped off to sleep and they caught me layin' there in the mornin'. After that, they double-chained me all the tighter and fed me even less. Which wasn't such a bad thing, what with that food bein' so awful it was likely doin' me more harm than good anyhow.

Figured by that time I'd likely die there.

TWENTY-FIVE

Independence, Mo.

Allan J. Pinkerton
Pinkerton National Detective Agency
Chicago, Ill.

Sir:

Concerning my ongoing investigation on behalf of our client Wm. Boggs, I write to report my imminent departure from this place and apprise you of my findings and plans.

Having spent several days in and around Jackson County, I am confident I have exhausted the sources of information here. Little to nothing is available in the way of reliable records. The official files are either misplaced or destroyed or never existed.

An interview with the man who was sheriff at the time was helpful in reconstructing the crime. He admits his investigation was insufficient owing to inclement weather, public interference, political pressure, &c. &c. but remains confident in his original conclusion that Orrin Porter Rockwell, whose name has been associated with the crime both at the time and ever since and has been mentioned throughout my investigations, is the guilty party. That the late Joseph Smith,

142

leader of the Mormon religion to which Rockwell belongs, ordered the crime is likewise firm in his mind. The former lawman is yet troubled by his inability to bring either of the accused to justice.

Also still in this area is the attorney who represented Rockwell in the affair, and he too consented to talk to me. Mr. Alexander Doniphan (a person of some import in Missouri) holds views that are somewhat different, as you might imagine. While he offered no opinion, even when prompted, as to the guilt or innocence of his former client, I am of the impression that he does not doubt the possibility of his guilt—in fact, my suspicion is that he may well believe it a fact. However, he was very lawyerly in the manner in which he provided information and holds to the notion that if the grand jury could not be convinced there was sufficient evidence on which to indict the accused, then the result at trial would have been a foregone conclusion had the government had the wherewithal to force the issue in the courts.

I shall embark on the morrow for Salt Lake City in Utah Territory. I anticipate no objective information in the Mormon stronghold but believe that going there is the next logical step in this inquiry, and I feel obligated to pursue suspicions concerning Porter Rockwell and the Latter-day Saints as far as practical or possible. Perhaps some disaffected individuals with knowledge of the affair can be located and encouraged to talk. My intention, at the very least, is to confront Rockwell with the evidence against him and solicit his comment.

Thank you, sir, for the funds forwarded to this place. The balance still in my possession should be adequate to see me through to Salt Lake City and establish myself there. While I have not had occasion to organize my expense receipts, I hope your trust in me is sufficient to send additional money there. I cannot say how long my stay will be, nor can I say at this time whether a visit to our client in California to present my findings will be advisable. I will, of course, consult with you concerning that decision before it is made.

Until then, I remain your humble servant,
s/Calvin Pogue

———◆———

Independence, Mo.

William M. Boggs
Napa, Calif.

My Dear Bill,

For the past several days I have been here in Independence pursuing information relevant to my investigation of the attempted assassination of your late father. Tomorrow I leave for Utah Territory to make further inquiries.

Being here has given me a clearer understanding of the circumstances of the crime. I have visited your old family home and talked with people who have firsthand knowledge of and involvement with those unfortunate events of long ago.

Prior to my time in Missouri I visited Springfield and Nauvoo in Illinois, pursuing information concerning the possible involvement of Joseph Smith and the Mormons, including Orrin Porter Rockwell.

I feel compelled to say to you that while my inquiries have been helpful, I have failed to uncover anything new or earthshaking. However, what I have learned seems, to me, to support some obvious conclusions that I will share with you at the appropriate juncture.

We appreciate your patience throughout the course of this case as well as the trust you have placed in the Pinkerton Detective Agency.

Respectfully yours,
s/Calvin Pogue
Pinkerton Nat'l Detective Agency

———————◆———————

The transcontinental railroad, under construction since the summer of 1865, aided, as he had hoped, Pogue's trip West. While the eastbound Central Pacific inched through the Sierra, the Union Pacific comparatively raced across the prairie by the mile. Pogue rode the rails as far as Cheyenne, in Wyoming Territory, which got him within 440 miles of Salt Lake City in relative comfort.

But the rest of the trip tested his tolerance for pain as he jounced and jostled over the mountains and plains in a succession of Concord coaches, mud wagons, and stagecoaches of indeterminate type and manufacture. After the lurching incline up Sherman Summit, the choking Red Desert dust, the sagebrush monotony surrounding Fort Bridger, and the bone-jarring carom down Echo Canyon, all while loaded down with insipid home station meals and weighty exhaustion from vermin-infested bunks, Pogue almost believed he could see in the tidy streets of Salt Lake City the Zion the Mormons proclaimed it to be.

He lowered himself stiffly from the coach at the station in the city's commercial district, feeling his game leg hit the ground all the way to the top of his throbbing head. Carrying his valise but leaving the carpetbag and trunk for later pickup, he hobbled across the wide street and hauled himself up the steps with the handrail on the porch of the Salt Lake House.

After arranging delivery of his baggage, he purchased a flask of whiskey and retired to his room. He intended to massage his knee with liniment, ease the rest of his body with an infusion of alcohol, and then sleep as long as he was able—setting aside hunger, ablutions, and work for another day.

———————◆———————

Day finally came that Alexander Doniphan got me back into court. The judge—different one, this time—asked was I guilty of jailbreak, to which question we answered no. So he put up a jury, and

145

Doniphan argued every way he could think of on my defense.

He said I shouldn't have been locked up in the first place on account of there weren't enough evidence of my havin' shot Lilburn Boggs to bring me to trial. He said there couldn't have been no jail-break on account of we never broke down no door nor jimmied no lock. He said some other things too, none of which convinced that judge.

But the jury must've thought he had somethin'. For while they came back with a verdict of guilty, they sentenced me to five minutes in the county jail as punishment.

If I thought I was a free man, which I did, I was again disappointed. Sheriff Reynolds and that other judge who'd kept me locked up all along kept me jailed all night long while they scrounged around for some other legal nonsense they could use to keep me. I don't doubt that Boggs was in on it too.

Anyhow, they couldn't come up with nothin', and come the mornin' they let me go. Eighth day of December it was, 1843. I'd been near nine months locked up and was glad to be free.

TWENTY-SIX

CALVIN POGUE SLEPT AWAY the rest of the day and deep into the night before awakening stiff and sore and hungry. Stripping off his travel-worn clothes, he bathed as thoroughly as possible with a cake of lye soap, china wash basin, and pitcher of tepid water. He dumped the soiled water in the chamber pot and refilled the basin to shave.

Feeling almost human again after covering himself from the skin out with wrinkled but fresh clothing, the investigator lowered himself down the staircase stiff-legged. He rapped the heavy room key on the desk to awaken the snoring desk clerk and asked about the possibility of finding something to eat.

"This late? Not likely," the night man said, mopping up chin drool with a shirtsleeve. "Any respectable place has been shut up for hours."

"How about someplace disrespectable?"

He seemed to consider the question as he finished wiping up with the palm his hand. "Go south a block, then east half a block. Then right, down a little alley—Commercial Street, it is. Mind yourself. Hoodlums have been known to frequent the area. Street's lined with houses offering any number of activities forbidden by Moses.

"Halfway down is a putrid little saloon in a space the size of a broom closet. I am told it never closes and that a flyblown free lunch is ever available on the sideboard. Wouldn't know from personal experience, of course. But so I am told."

The place was exactly where it was said to be, and very nearly as described. A slender bar ran half the length of the room, with space for a half dozen or so drinkers to prop and bend elbows. No one stood there at present. In fact, the bartender, in a cramped passageway on the business side of the bar, appeared to be the room's only occupant. Through dim lantern light and haze, Pogue spotted the sideboard on the narrow back wall. And, indeed, it held something resembling food. At least from a distance.

As his gaze worked its way back up the room, past the two small tables that filled the space beyond the bar, the detective noticed a man, seated in deep shadow against the wall, his hand around a whiskey glass on the table in front of him. Pogue dropped a handful of coins on the bar, ordered a beer, and asked about the food.

"Yours if you want it. It ain't exactly fresh at this hour, but I don't guess it'll kill you. Leastways, no more than usual."

With slivers and slices of cold ham, a couple of hard biscuits, a pickle, and a brined boiled egg on a plate, Pogue started back toward his beer on the bar.

"Why the limp?" the shadowed man at the table asked.

The Pinkerton man stopped, studied the man, and went on. He gnawed a bite from the edge of a biscuit, fingered up a hunk of ham to follow it, and chased the gob down with a swig of beer.

"Why the limp?"

Pogue placed the beer glass on the bar and turned toward the man. "Who wants to know?"

"I'm guessing you got shot."

After taking a bite out of the pickle—a limp and unsatisfying pickle, as it turned out—he picked up the plate and the beer and took a seat across from the man, sliding the stiff leg straight beside the table. The man had tousled hair and a gaunt whiskered face, and his wide, wild eyes had a haunted look.

"Good guess," Pogue said.

"War?"

"That's right. Not so hard to guess, though, that one."

"Maybe. We don't see too many war wounds here in Zion."

"Why?"

The man said the late war was all but nonexistent in Utah Territory. Unique among the states and territories that did not secede, Utah sent no troops to the war. Brigham Young, he said, routinely prophesied the collapse of the nation even as he feigned support for the Union. The Mormon leader also did all in his power—which was considerable—to make life difficult for the US Army troops billeted on the hillside above the city. Brother Brigham controlled trade with Camp Douglas, forbade his followers from interacting with the soldiers, and interfered with federal officials in any and every way he could conceive.

"How is it you know so much about Brigham Young and his doings?"

The man laughed and rose from the table. "Stick around, soldier. We'll talk more once I'm back. Call of nature," he said as he hobbled toward the door.

"Why the limp?" Pogue called out.

"Got shot."

TWENTY-SEVEN

MEAGER FARE THOUGH IT WAS, the free lunch satisfied Pogue's appetite. He decided to have another beer and await the mystery man. If he wasn't back by the time he finished the beer, the detective figured he would walk the dark city streets for a few hours before returning to his room to plan the day's itinerary.

Halfway down the glass, his chance companion returned, limping his way to the table and retaking his seat in the shadows, back to the wall.

"So, you were shot," Pogue said.

"Shot in the hip. Nearly killed me. I lived, but I'll live with it till I die. This limp, I mean. Hurts like mad, besides."

"How did it happen?"

"At the hand of a young renegade name of Lot Huntington. He was a friend of mine, of sorts. I was a semiofficial lawman at the time. One of Brother Brigham's boys, you might say. Lot was a good boy, but he had this thing about stealing horses. Tried to take him in, and he decided to shoot it out."

"Did you shoot him?"

"No. Could have killed him. Should have, I guess. But, as I said, the boy was a friend of mine. I didn't think he would draw on me in the middle of the day in the city streets, but he did. On Christmas Day, no less.

"He ended up getting shot for a horse thief anyway, a couple of years later. Killed by Porter Rockwell."

Pogue perked up at the mention of the name. "Rockwell? You know Rockwell?"

The man laughed. "Yes. Me and Port go back more'n thirty years, I guess."

"You intrigue me, sir. Can I buy you a drink and engage you in conversation?"

The man looked him over as he thought it over. "I don't believe we've met yet."

Pogue extended a hand across the table. "I'm Calvin Pogue, of Chicago. Visiting your city on business."

The handshake was accepted with a vicelike grip. "Hickman. William Hickman. Like any number of other Williams out West here, I'm sometimes called Wild Bill."

"It is a pleasure to meet you, Mr. Hickman. Please, tell me about yourself. May I take notes?"

"What for? You one of them writers? Them fellows that write them dime novels are always finagling to get my story, but they never want to make it worth my while. You one of them?"

Pogue said, "I assure you I'm not, Mr. Hickman. I do record a good deal of information from people in my line of work, but I am by no means a writer."

"All right, then. What, exactly, is your line of work?"

"I'll be happy to tell you, sir, but right now I'm much more interested in listening than talking. Before we part, I promise to tell you all."

"Good enough," Hickman said. Then he launched into a tale that kept Pogue scribbling furiously.

◆

William A. "Wild Bill" Hickman was nearing sixty years of age when encountered by Calvin Pogue, Pinkerton man. He had joined with the Mormons in Missouri and had been with them since. He followed the flock to Nauvoo, Illinois, and then westward to Salt Lake City. Over the years he had managed to accumulate, in the Mormon fashion, a number of wives. He had married ten times, fathered thirty-five children. Lately he had strayed from the Saints and was visiting the city somewhat on the sly the night he met the detective.

Much to Pogue's delight, Hickman had been linked with Orrin Porter Rockwell during all those years among the Mormons.

Both had been named Danite chiefs, widely feared on the frontier and accused of numerous crimes. Both had been bodyguards to Joseph Smith, an assignment that continued with Brigham Young when he took over leadership of the Saints. According to Hickman, both men had been among "Brigham's Boys," a loose-knit and ever-changing group of rough and tough men willing to do the man's bidding, no matter the nature of the assignment.

And, Hickman said, those assignments often involved the shedding of blood.

He said, "We was both lawmen, me and Port, appointed by Brigham Young. I suppose I still am since I've never been told otherwise or offered an official release of any kind. Once Utah became a territory, that made us deputy US marshals. Not just me and Port—Brigham had lots more like us. But I guess the two of us were at it longer and more often than the rest of them. And we did lots more than act as enforcers for the prophet too."

"Such as?"

"Tried to keep the peace with the Indians. Escorted people and livestock and freight on the trails in and out of Utah. Acted as explorers and guides and hunters. Went to the mining districts in California and South Pass to see what wealth we could acquire for the Church.

"During the difficulties running up to the arrival of General Albert Sidney Johnston and the United States Army here back in '57, Brother Brigham got a contract from the government to carry the mail. Formed an outfit called the YX Company, as in Young Express, which me and Port was part of. Each of us had a route on the way to Missouri till the government pulled the contract.

"When the army was on the march, we pulled 'em up short

out on the plains east of Fort Bridger. Me and Port and Lot Smith each had a band of raiders. We burnt wagon trains of supplies, rustled livestock, caused all kinds of trouble. I personally set the torch to Fort Bridger so's the army couldn't use it as winter quarters. Wasn't much blood shed in that war, but I spilled a little. Shot a spy, name of Yates. Some wasn't too happy about my doing that, I'll tell you.

"But he wasn't the first, last, or only man I killed in service to Brigham Young. I could curl your hair with some of them stories.

"Later on, during the War Between the States, another army was sent here, and we let 'em come. By that time, me and Brigham Young wasn't seeing eye-to-eye on a number of things—such as my getting fair compensation for all the dirty work I'd done on his behalf. So when I took up with that army commander, Colonel Connor, that was all she wrote for me and the Mormons. That didn't pay off so well either, working for him. But that's another story."

"I'd enjoy hearing it, Mr. Hickman. But first, tell me more, if you will, about Rockwell. You said part of your duties—and, I assume, his—included killing. Is that so? Was Rockwell a 'hired' killer, so to speak?"

Again, Hickman laughed as if Pogue had told a joke.

———◆———

Bein' out of jail didn't mean I's off the hook. There I was, penniless and half-starved and in Jackson County, Missouri, where most folks would as soon kill me as look at me. Plenty of them pukes tried before I got out of that godforsaken place.

My mother and I started out together, but there was so many stories around sayin' mobbers was out to get me, to see I didn't get out of there alive, that before the day was out I sent her on ahead alone, figurin' she'd be safer without me.

I headed northeast for Nauvoo, keepin' off the roads, travelin' mostly by night. Now and then I'd see mobs ridin' by, and from time to time I'd overhear 'em askin' folks along the road if I'd been seen thereabouts. Some settlers stood me to a meal now and again, and some even gave me the loan of a few dollars.

Bein' barefoot, I soon wore the soles off my feet and got to where I couldn't hardly get along at all. This farmer gave me leave to ride his horse to the next town. Cost me half a dollar but bought me fourteen miles. Another day I's so wore out I paid another man six bits to carry me in his wagon for a time. But most of the way I hoofed it.

It went on that way for better'n two weeks till I finally caught a ferry ride across the big river and showed up in Nauvoo at Christmastime. Joseph was celebratin' a party with a passel of folks at the Mansion House, all decked out in their finery. I nearly had to beat the man at the door to get in, and then a bunch of others laid hands on me to throw me back out. Can't say as I blame them, lookin' back. I hadn't hardly bathed in weeks, had nigh onto a year's growth on my hair and beard, and had hundreds of miles of Missouri dirt ground into what was left of my clothes.

Joseph came over to see what the trouble was. He considered I must be a poor wanderin' drunk, but it bein' Christmas and all, he said I wasn't to be turned away without first bein' fed a proper meal. Finally he saw my face through all the dirt. "Orrin Porter Rockwell!" he hollered out, and from then on I was the belle of the ball, toasted with more wine than I'd seen in a good long time and enjoyin' the company of friends I'd not seen for years. Seems ever' one of them wanted to hear my story, and I told it over and again till I was tired out.

It was about that time that Joseph saw fit to bless me, and he pronounced a prophecy on me. He said I needn't fear no enemy so long as I was loyal to the faith. And he said, "Cut not thy hair and no bullet or blade can harm thee!"

Now, I don't know what got into him to make such a promise on the Lord's name. But his words have proved true up till now.

Anyways, prophecy or not, I was glad to be back in Joseph's company and out of the clutches of Boggs.

TWENTY-EIGHT

ONCE THE LAUGHTER was contained, Hickman said, "I cannot begin to count, Mr. Pogue, the number of men Porter Rockwell killed. Some lawful killings, others foul murders. Most on orders from Brigham Young, many on Port's own hook. Given that I've fallen out of favor around here, I wouldn't doubt the man's got orders to do me in."

"Tell me about some of those killings."

"Some I ain't sure of the truth of the matter—like me, dozens of killings has been hung on him that he had nothing to do with. If Port's orders from on high were like mine, and I don't doubt they were, some were commanded and happened and nobody knows about them and never will. But some of the deaths are well known—and some of them I have on good authority who was behind them.

"One time on the way back from California, as I was told by men who were there, he killed an Indian who tried to bluff his way into camp in the dark of the moon. Fooled everybody but Port, who shot him down. 'Course anybody with any sand would've done that killing, so it don't hardly count.

"They say some pilgrim coming through here on the way to California—this would've been in '50, maybe '51—was a mobber who'd been in on the killing of Joseph Smith back in Illinois, or

ROD MILLER

so it was told around. Port got up a posse and run him to ground out in the desert, and word was he cut the man's head off.

"'Bout that same time, there was this apostate Mormon name of Al Babbit who was secretary of the territorial government. Port had escorted him and a party of others back to the states for various kinds of dealings. Babbit was on his way back in a fast carriage with a load of mail and tens of thousands of dollars on his person, government money for territorial business. Him and his shotgun guards got themselves butchered in Ash Hollow out Nebraska way. 'Most everyone laid that one on Indians, and maybe it was. But some claimed Port showed up at Fort Laramie soon after with Babbit's teams among his stock and some of the man's papers on his person.

Hickman told of another bloody incident laid at Rockwell's feet, one that aroused a good deal of public outrage and persistent legal scrutiny.

A band of California gamblers arrived in the territory late in 1857, presumably to set up shop and skin the soldiers due to arrive there with the Utah Expedition. But Brigham Young would have none of it—considering any advantage taken of the troops to be his responsibility—and ordered the unsavory characters held on house arrest for weeks. Then Rockwell and a fellow ruffian were given orders to escort four of the gamblers—two of them brothers named Aiken—out of Utah on the southern trail to California.

The guards attacked their charges, it was alleged, at a campsite some one hundred miles south of Salt Lake City. Rockwell blamed it on Indians. One prisoner, shot in the back, escaped in the dark. The other three were knocked on the head and dumped into the Sevier River. Two of them floated away, dead, but one of the Aiken brothers survived and stumbled into the nearby town of Salt Creek, bloody, half-dressed, and half-dead. The man who had been shot also found his way back to the town.

Unfortunately for them, Rockwell was still in the neighborhood and knew of their arrival. Town leaders conscripted two young men to haul the wounded men back to Salt Lake City. But, by design, it was believed, Rockwell waylaid the party along the

156

road and made good on his earlier attempt to kill the men, this time employing a shotgun for the task and dumping the bodies into a spring-fed pond.

"Not two months later, Port was at it again," Hickman said. "This one, like that Aiken affair, caused quite a fuss. Word was, a fellow name of Henry Jones was making nasty with his mother, if you can imagine such a disgusting thing. Church leaders, of course, couldn't allow such depravity and sent Port to put a stop to it.

"Him and some of his boys lured Henry out of town and sliced off his offending parts right to the quick, figuring that would solve the problem. But Brigham, or someone, figured he had ought to die for such a grievous sin, and his mother likewise. But the two of them had quit the country already and were running south.

"Port caught up with them down around Payson, hiding out in an abandoned dugout. Slit the woman's throat, shot Henry Jones, pulled the roof down on them, caved off the walls, and called it a good-enough grave."

Pogue asked, "Was there no arrest for those killings? No public outcry for justice?"

Hickman laughed. "Not a chance of any such thing happening. Whether he ordered it personally or not, word was at the time that Brigham Young wanted it done. That rumor alone—again, never mind the truth of it—was enough to discourage anyone in the territory from raising any kind of stink about it, fearing the same fate for themselves if they did. Like I told you, Brother Brigham had—still has—his fingers in everything, and them fingers often form into an iron fist."

Hickman's stories continued without pause.

John Gheen, a Salt Lake City butcher, fell out of favor with the Mormons, Hickman said, and was shot down by Rockwell in the city streets. "He was shot in the forehead. Died with a gun in his hand. There were no eyewitnesses. Police ruled it a suicide." He laughed. "Never mind there were no powder burns, or that folks who heard the ruckus said there were two shots fired."

And another.

"Port had himself a roadhouse down at the south end of the valley for years. Closed it down not long ago—last year, maybe the year before, I don't know. One night a bullwhacker for Johnston's army stopped by there on his way out to Camp Floyd. This would have been in '59. Anyway, there was some uproar in the bar when this fellow got drunk and disorderly. Port threw him out after beating on him, and the man went on his way.

"Not long after, Port rode out to tend to some business he had in Lehi, a town down that way where Rockwell kept a house. Few miles down the road, this teamster was laying for him and would not lay off Port. So he shot the rude fool in the bread box and turned himself over to the law. Being a righteous killing, nothing came of it."

The storyteller finally stopped and told Pogue his overworked vocal cords needed lubrication. The detective fetched another glass of beer for each of them, along with a whiskey for Hickman. The beer went down in a long gulp; he nursed the whiskey as his tales continued. Pogue hoisted the foot of his throbbing leg onto the seat of an empty chair and settled in for another round of rapid note-taking.

"There was this big bear of a man named Joachim Johnston who made his living stealing from the army. Went in cahoots with a couple of other fellows to counterfeit government pay vouchers. All well and good until they got caught and one of them tried to lay it off on Brigham Young. Said he set them up in business and offered protection for a share of the profits—and simply for the upset it would cause the army.

"So, one night Johnston and one of the others—Myron Brewer, if memory serves—got all liquored up and were staggering home. Died on the street from a dose of buck and ball," Hickman said and then laughed. "Official report was that they killed each other! Can't say for sure, but there were rumors Rockwell did the deed on Brigham's orders to punish them outlaws for their indiscretion."

There was another double killing about that same time, Hickman said. This one was, without doubt, the work of Porter

THE ASSASSINATION OF GOVERNOR BOGGS

Rockwell. A deputized member of a posse, Rockwell pursued the
McRae brothers, wanted for robbery, up Emigration Canyon.
The bandits, despite being cornered and without hope of escape,
refused to surrender—or so it was said. The deputy shotgunned
them into submission. There was some disagreement over whether
the boys were armed at the time. Their mother said later that
Rockwell dumped the bodies at her doorstep with the complaint
that she had been negligent in her duties as parent to the pair.

Hickman sipped his whiskey, licked his lips, fixed his unwav-
ering gaze on his audience, and launched another tale.

"Hold up, Mr. Hickman," Pogue said as he finished filling
another of many pages and turned to a fresh one. "How many
more of these killings are there?"

"Depends on who you ask," Hickman said. "Those who don't
like him say Port has dozens, scores of victims to his credit. I
heard him once accused of one hundred deaths. That's rubbish.
But there are plenty. Just one of the hazards of this line of work."

"And you've no doubt that these killings—some of them, at
least—were at the behest of leaders of the Mormon church."

"Sure as I'm sitting here. As I said, Port and me were in the
same line of work, working for the same people. We both did our
jobs and did them well. Me, I'm out of it. But not Port, he's still
one of Brigham's boys."

"Let me ask you something, Mr. Hickman. I have been told
that Rockwell shot Lilburn Boggs in Missouri, back in 1842. And
that he did it on orders from Joseph Smith. Are either or both of
those things true?"

Hickman did not blink or otherwise show surprise at the
question. But the furrows in his forehead and slant of his eyebrows
signaled displeasure. "Why would you ask me that? What's your
game, anyway?"

Dropping his propped leg to the floor and pulling himself
upright in his chair, Pogue folded his notebook closed and said,
"Mr. Hickman, I trust you are familiar with the Pinkerton Detective Agency."

The supposition drew a nod.

"I am an investigator for the firm. My assignment, at present, is to determine who was responsible for the attempted killing of Governor Boggs. Not as a legal matter, you understand. Our investigation is in service to a private party."

Hickman tossed back the contents of his whiskey glass and set the glass down with more force than necessary. The furrows in his brow deepened, and his light gray eyes seemed almost to glow through the dim as his stare penetrated Pogue.

"Understand this, Pinkerton man. There's no love lost between me and Porter Rockwell nowadays. As I said, it would not surprise me if he walked in the door this very minute and shot me dead. I may well be on the man's list of things to do.

"But know this, as well. I will not, and would not under any circumstances, allow some two-bit detective who is only in it for the money to use me to get the goods on another man, no matter who, what, or why. I suggest you remove yourself from my presence immediately, Mr. Pogue, or I may well forget that I am no longer in the killing business."

Pogue met the man's stare, but facing down Hickman's icy wrath was not easy. "I'm sorry if I've offended you, Mr. Hickman. I assure you, it was not my intention. But I will not be bullied." An ominous ratcheting of metal echoed under the table as the detective drew back the hammer on the short-barreled pistol he'd pulled from the holster on his belt. "Any violence toward me will be returned with pleasure."

"Put your gun away, Pogue. You have nothing to fear from me. But you'll get no more from me either. If you want to hang the Boggs shooting on Porter Rockwell, you'll do it with none of my assistance. Now get out of my sight before I change my mind."

Pogue lowered the hammer on the revolver with a click but kept the gun in his hand as he rose from the chair and made his way to the door. Just before he stepped into the street, he turned back to the man in the shadows.

"One more question, Mr. Hickman. Would it surprise you if I discover that Rockwell did, indeed, pull the trigger on Boggs?"

For the last time, he heard Wild Bill Hickman's sarcastic laugh.

From the time I got back to Nauvoo and among my people, I made it my job to forget about Lilburn Boggs and Missouri. Fact is, though, all my time in Nauvoo I slept with one eye open, ever alert for Missouri pukes.

I worked at this and that but mostly acted as one of Joseph's body-guards, for there was always enemies about, both from Missouri and by now our neighbors in Illinois too. There was even some of the Saints that turned against Joseph, and they was as bad as any.

They killed him in June of '44.

There wasn't a thing I could do about it. He was locked up in the Carthage jail, under guard by the militia—so-called—when a black-faced mob gunned him down.

After that, it got hot around them parts. As bad as Missouri. 'Most all of us Mormons threw in with Brigham Young, and when we was finally run out of Illinois in '46, we followed him west. We stayed north of Missouri, but from time to time dropped down into settlements to trade.

I found out that all this time Boggs had been sleepin' with one eye open fearin' me or some other Mormon would show up and finish the job!

Boggs left Missouri in '46 to head west himself. Word was that he was afeared the whole trip, knowin' we was on the trail ourselves. I heard said a St. Louis newspaper wrote that we'd killed him some-wheres out on the plains. No such thing happened.

We never made it no farther than the Missouri River in '46 and had folks strung out all across Iowa at that. With just about every-thing we owned left behind in Nauvoo and no way to outfit that many folks for an overland journey, we just couldn't go no farther.

Boggs, we was told later, went all the way to California that year. First direct word I heard of him, though, was at Fort Laramie when we passed there in '47. He'd been by there the summer before. Man runnin' the place said Boggs told him to keep his livestock penned should the Mormons come by. Said we'd steal him blind otherwise.

What a scoundrel.

TWENTY-NINE

WHEN POGUE WALKED OUT of the bar and into Commercial Street, a ribbon of dawn already defined the craggy Wasatch Mountain peaks towering in the east. Each step he took sent shooting pains up and down his leg, stiff from hours sitting in the saloon. A walk through the silent streets of Salt Lake City would be just the thing to loosen it up a bit and calm the ache.

A few lights winked here and there with early risers, but for the most part the city spread in darkness into the valley. The shopping district was yet vacant, and the temple block lay empty. Large granite boulders littered the place, their various shapes showing progress from rock to squared-up building stone. The rising walls, bound by platforms and scaffolds, promised an impressive building in which the Mormon elders could marry women in droves in secret ceremonies.

A block to the east of the temple, he came to the Eagle Gate, entrance to Brigham Young's estate. A single room at the back of one of the buildings was lit, most likely a communal kitchen where fires were being laid to prepare the morning meal for the church leader's several wives and children.

Before the day was out, he hoped to obtain an audience with the man.

As he studied the buildings behind a low wall, a voice behind him said, "Is there something you're looking for?"

Pogue tensed, startled at the interruption, and turned quickly to find its source. But he found he could not move, as a powerful hand gripped his shoulder.

"Stand easy," he heard. "If that's a pistol under that lump in your jacket you'd best be handing it to me. No smart stuff, mind you."

Slowly and deliberately, the detective grasped the butt of the pistol between thumb and forefinger, slowly pulled it from under his jacket, and dangled it in front of him for his captor to reach around and take. He wondered just who had seized him and what the man's intentions were.

"Turn around now, nice and slow."

A slow exhalation of held breath signaled Pogue's relief at the sight of a police uniform.

"Now, suppose you tell me why you're lurkin' and snoopin' around here when decent folks ought to be abed."

"Just out for a walk, is all."

"Strange time for it, wouldn't you say?"

"It would seem so to most, I suppose," Pogue said. "But not an unusual occurrence for me, I assure you. A good night's sleep is something I rarely find. So, instead, I walk."

"From the smell of you, I'm more likely to believe you've been all night swilling beer. Come with me."

———◆———

The cell, at least, was clean. Small enough compensation for being locked up for four hours. Pogue sat alone and quiet on the cot, awaiting the arrival of a city police officer whose head performed some function beyond holding the ears apart.

The policeman who hauled him in had no interest in Pogue's story. Wouldn't look at his identification. Simply dumped that, along with the other contents of his pockets and his pistol, into a canvas bag that he shoved into a lockbox before showing the Pinkerton man to the cramped cage in the back corner of the room. The place seemed to be a neighborhood office and temporary lockup rather than a typical police station.

"You just sit here and sober up, mister. It's back on patrol for me."

"Listen," Pogue said, "I can explain. If you'll just allow me—"

The nightstick slammed into the bars, interrupting Pogue's plea.

"Save your breath. There's nothing you've got to say that I want to hear."

"Allow me, then, to speak to your superior."

The nightstick hit the bars again. "You see anybody else here, mister? Sleep it off. The boss'll be here by nine, depending on how much paperwork meets him at the city jail. Save it for him."

The sun was well up and the day underway when the policeman returned, accompanied by an older, heavyset man wearing a suit rather than a uniform.

"There he is, sir. That's the man I told you about."

The "sir" walked back to the cell and stopped, legs spread and hands clasped behind his back. He studied the man seated on the cot. Pogue returned the stare.

"So I guess you've got something to say."

The detective watched the man for a moment before replying. "Will it do me any good to talk to you, or will I need to speak to someone with authority to make decisions?"

"I am an assistant chief of police. I assure you I have the authority to lock up an impertinent sot such as yourself and forget for a good long time where he was put. Suppose you tell me why you were skulking about the Beehive House in the middle of the night."

"First of all, it wasn't the middle of the night. Early morning, more like. Second, I wasn't 'lurking' but merely out for a walk, as I told the officer."

"He said you stood there for some time, studying the place. Night or morning, it was an hour when anyone on the street is likely up to no good. Try again."

"It is as I said. I did look the place over, as I intend to stop by there today and seek an appointment with Brigham Young."

The chief's eyes widened momentarily. "You? A common

drunk seeking an audience with President Young? Absurd!"

"What is absurd is your assertion that I am a common drunk. I have not even been asked my identity. Had your subordinate followed basic police procedure and done so—not to mention practiced simple, common courtesy—I would not be here. Nor would you."

Pogue could see the man's neck flush. Through clenched teeth, he said, "So, then, who are you to be lecturing me on police procedure?"

"As my credentials clearly show, had anyone bothered to look at them, I am an investigator with the Pinkerton National Detective Agency. I suppose that you have heard of the firm, even in this isolated backwater."

"A Pinkerton man, eh? Well, that and a pocket watch will get you the time. Doesn't amount to diddly, so far as I'm concerned."

Nevertheless, he opened the lockbox and studied the identification papers. He removed the revolver from its holster and rotated the cylinder, checking each chamber and removing the cartridges. He shook the coins, jackknife, money clip, and other items that belonged in Pogue's pockets onto the desk.

"Suppose you tell me, Mr. Pogue, why you found it necessary to get your bearings in our city at such an ungodly hour."

Pogue slapped his left knee a few times and said, "This knee. It was shattered by a musket ball in the war and causes me a good deal of pain. I am often unable to sleep, so I walk."

"My man said you stank of beer and tobacco smoke."

"I was hungry when I awakened, and the only food available was a lunch counter in a saloon on Commercial Street. I did spend a good deal of time there conversing with a man who claimed he once enforced the law here. William Hickman, he said his name was."

"Hickman? He's in town? I believe he has been living for some time in Carson City. I shall inform my officers to be on the look-out for him. I suspect there are warrants for him. If not, there should be.

"I am inclined to say, Mr. Pogue, that spending time with

a scapegrace such as Bill Hickman does nothing in the way of convincing me of your good intentions toward my city and its people."

"Our meeting was strictly happenstance. One cripple reaching out to another, as it were," Pogue said. "He is a curious sort of man, your Wild Bill."

"Curious doesn't begin to describe him. But enough of that. Suppose you tell me the nature of your business here."

———————◆———————

Never gave Boggs much of a thought once we got to the Great Basin and put down stakes here by the Salt Lake. Seems I was hardly out of the saddle for months at a time, what with comin' here from the Missouri and then bein' sent by Brigham Young to scout around hereabouts, seein' what was here and what our prospects was.

After a few weeks of that, I was sent east to find out about the big company of Saints that took to the trail behind us. Found the first of them at Deer Creek, went on near as far as the North Platte till I had accounted for them all.

Then I turned back toward the Salt Lake Valley and home, such as it was. Whilst I was all that time a-horseback, see, the Saints was takin' plots and lots and settlin' in for winter. Me, I got some credit for the work I done but was behind in settlin' in and wanted to get to it.

But Brother Brigham, he was on his way back to the Winter Quarters on the Missouri by then, and we met up in Echo Canyon, just a few days out of Salt Lake. He turned me around again, wantin' me to hunt for his party for a time. So I traveled with them back to the Sweetwater and then turned around again for home.

Then, just about the time winter started to set in, in November, the head men of the church here decided we'd run short of supplies before summer and had best lay in what we could from California.

California, of course, that was where Boggs had gone to. Crossin' trails with him wasn't high on my list. Still, I was one who was chosen to make the trip to California and bring back supplies.

THIRTY

IT TOOK A GOOD DEAL of time and countless interruptions, but the assistant police chief was finally satisfied with Calvin Pogue's explanation of his presence in Salt Lake City.

"If it's a warm welcome you're hoping for, I fear you will be disappointed," the policeman said.

"If ever I had any such notion, Mr. Hickman relieved me of it right away. Your officer only served to reinforce the unwelcoming ways of Salt Lake City."

"That should not surprise you, detective, since your stated intention here seems to be the slander of one of our citizens."

"Slander? I have no idea what you're talking about. I am a professional investigator, here for the sole purpose of gathering information. Our investigation's purpose is to reveal the truth. How that can be interpreted as slander is beyond me."

"Rather than truth, you appear to be pursuing Porter Rockwell in a misguided attempt to hang a long-dead crime on him. A crime for which the State of Missouri vindicated him all those years ago."

"While it is true my inquiries at present focus on Rockwell, that is only because the evidence gathered to date requires it. Neither he nor anyone else here has anything to fear. I might add that Rockwell was hardly 'vindicated' as you say. The fact that the legal system found insufficient evidence on which to indict him is certainly no indication of his innocence. As an officer of the law, you are surely aware that a legal finding of guilt or innocence often has no bearing on whether or not the suspect committed a crime."

"True, Mr. Pogue, but also irrelevant. How long ago was this attempted assassination? Twenty years? Twenty-five? More? The statute of limitations has long since expired, so even if you find enough evidence against Port, there would be no legal recourse,"

"It is not legal recourse I am interested in. Just the truth. Our client in this matter wants to know, finally, who was responsible."

"And just who is your client, Mr. Pogue?"

"Normally I would tell you that is none of your business. But, in this instance, I would not violate any confidence by saying that the Pinkerton Agency was engaged to investigate this matter by the family of Governor Boggs."

"Tarnation! Lilburn Boggs single-handedly caused more grief to this people than any other person in our history. Is it never enough? Will his family continue to persecute us?"

"I cannot say for certain what the intentions of the Boggs family are, sir. But I can say with confidence that persecution of the Mormon people is not their purpose. Now, may I go about my business?"

"I will release you, but don't plan on leaving Salt Lake City just yet. I will consult with President Young for guidance as to what to do with you."

"What? President Young? What has he to do with this? He is not a public official, holds no government position, elected or otherwise, in this city or the territory. He is nothing more than a private citizen."

The chief laughed. "As you will, Mr. Pogue. But rest assured that regardless of the opinions or appointments of the federal government, Brigham Young is the man in charge around here. It is he who makes the decisions—whether regarding the Church, the government, the community, whatever."

"As I told you earlier, I hope to speak with Mr. Young myself. Perhaps, since he is to decide my fate anyway, you could arrange an audience with him and I can plead my own case."

"Just don't attempt to leave town until you hear from me, Mr. Pogue."

"Not to worry, chief. I have people to see."

———————◆———————

A haircut, shave, and hot bath at the hotel washed away the saloon and the cell and reinvigorated the detective. After a breakfast in a downtown eatery, he set out on the streets again, intending to see the city in daylight.

He browsed a bookshop, purchased a supply of collars in a haberdashery, and sampled the wares in a candy store. After watching what appeared to be hundreds of men scurrying around like so many ants at the temple block construction site, he ducked into a leather goods shop.

Saddles and harnesses lined the walls and filled the selling space, but he was drawn to a display table against the back wall. There, among a selection of belts and billfolds, stood a toy horse. The hide of the red speckled cow from which it was made produced a perfect representation of a sorrel and white pinto horse. A flowing mane and tail trimmed from the mane hair of a sorrel horse of nearly identical shade completed the color scheme. Pogue studied the animal: the tiny, stitched-on glass eyes and the stiff, thick black leather that formed the hooves, and the soft split-hide muzzle with painted nostrils.

The cashier asked if he would like to see a saddle for the horse and produced from under the counter a miniature stock saddle, pieced together from leather just as if it were full size. Skirts, fenders, fork, stirrup leathers, tiny oxbow stirrups carved from wood and covered with tapaderos, latigo straps, and a cinch of braided string—the saddle was accurate in every detail. Hanging from the horn was a tiny headstall made from whang leather.

Pogue carried his purchase back to his room and scratched out a letter on hotel stationery. His next stop was the post office.

ROD MILLER

THE SALT LAKE HOUSE
HOTEL-RESTAURANT-PUBLIC ROOM

Darling Emily Elizabeth,

I am in Salt Lake City in Utah Territory. It is a beautiful city, with tall mountains all around. Some of the mountains still have snow on the tops. There is also a big lake outside of town. It is not as big as Lake Michigan by Chicago, but this lake is very salty. It has no fish in it, and they say if you try to swim in it, you float and cannot sink. I have not been to the lake to try it, but that is what they say.

This beautiful pinto horse also comes from Salt Lake City, as does his tack. As you see, the saddle fits him perfectly. I believe he will make a beautiful addition to your stable. I will be interested to hear the name you choose for this remarkable horse.

I miss you, Emily Elizabeth, more every day—more than I can stand. I hope to leave here within a few days and to be home soon to see you again. It is also my hope, if at all possible, to stay with you there for a long, long time. Perhaps you will employ me as your "wrangler" to help care for your horse herd.

Until then, Please obey your mother and be the good girl I know you are.

Love always,
Father

———◆———

California was a big place, and if I ever had any cares about encounterin' Boggs there, I needn't have worried. Leastways not on that first trip out there in the winter of '47 and '48.

That was quite a trip, I'm here to say.

'Course with winter comin' on, we wasn't about to head west or north to meet up with the usual trail. Sam Brannan had come over

from San Francisco that way early on in the summer, and he knowed all about them Reeds and Donners that Boggs had been travelin' with what froze up and died in them mountains. So we knowed better than to try that. That Fremont soldier and his men had wrote of a trail to the southern part of California and said that them Spanish had a pack train trail down south. That's the way we went.

If ever there was much of a road, it wasn't much of one by then. We was off it and lookin' for it more than we was on it. We run short of grub and was eatin' our pack animals before even we got to Las Vegas, a waterin' hole and pastureland out in the desert that wasn't but halfway there. Finally we made it to this rancho called Chino along about Christmastime.

Some of our Battalion boys was there, who had marched off with the army from back in Iowa to fight the Mexicans. They was strung out up and down California, and I found out from them that Boggs was up north somewheres called Sonoma and was some sort of a muckety-muck up there, like a judge or some such. So I quit wonderin' about him and started wonderin' on how to get our outfit back home.

See, the man who was supposedly in charge of that trip weren't nothin' but a fool, and him and me didn't much see eye to eye. We'd bought us a couple hundred head of cattle, and he was hot to trot 'em on up the trail to home. But me, I knowed there wasn't no show in that idea as there wasn't enough grass anywhere near that trail we just come down to keep a herd half that size alive.

So when he went on in February despite my advice, I didn't. Me, I went down to San Diego to wait a spell before startin' home. Along about April, when I figured there'd maybe be enough graze to allow animals to make the trip, I and twenty-five of our Battalion boys left out of there with a herd of mules and a wagon filled with goods, which I drove the whole of the way, me bein' the first ever to take a wagon on that route.

We got through in fifty-five days, every man of us and every one of them mules.

Found out when we got home that that herd of cattle had dwindled to one scrawny bull by the time it got through, every one of the others starved and dead on the trail, and the men nearly so. Even still, some of them churchmen chastised me for not comin' along with them. Some even said the blame ought to be laid on me, as I ought to have guided them to grass that wasn't there. But I figured I tried to tell them and there wasn't much more I could've done, short of shootin' somebody for effect.

I wanted nothin' more by that time than to settle in and make myself a place. But that weren't to be.

THIRTY-ONE

THE POST OFFICE DOOR had hardly closed behind the Pinkerton investigator when a uniformed police officer approached.

"Are you Calvin Pogue?"

After pausing just long enough to create discomfort, Pogue told the policeman yes and then asked why he wanted to know.

"You're to come with me, sir."

"Why?"

"Couldn't say, sir. We were only told to find you."

"We?"

"Yes, sir. Me and three others. They're looking elsewhere."

"Am I under arrest?"

"No, sir. I'm not to take you to jail. I'm supposed to escort you to the Beehive House."

That revelation surprised Pogue. Then it troubled him. Was he being taken to Brigham Young's place of business for the requested interview, or did the president of the Mormons have something else in mind for him? He stewed on the possibilities as they walked the few blocks.

The Beehive House stood on a street corner next to the Eagle Gate, entrance to Young's estate. The gate was a metal arch across the street, atop which was a sculpture of a soaring eagle covered in bronze. The house itself was a large, two-story affair, where it was said Young lived with a number of his wives and many children. A small room, just beyond an entryway inside the front door, served as the Mormon leader's unofficial office. The house was named for a beehive atop a cupola on the roof—the beehive, Pogue knew, was a symbol of sorts used by the Saints but he did not know why.

Adjacent to the Beehive House to the west was a larger building, not quite so ornate, called the Lion House. This, he believed, served as residence for yet more wives and children of Brigham—the "Lion of the Lord."

The policeman passed Pogue off to another man at the door to the Beehive House; his size and demeanor marked him as a likely bodyguard and protector. Once inside, the man asked Pogue if he was armed and if he would mind being searched. The detective answered the first question in the affirmative, the second in the negative, carefully handing the man his small revolver and then extending his arms for a cursory pat down.

The office was small and informal. A writing table with a wooden chair sat near a west-facing window. Against another wall stood a rolltop desk and swivel chair, in which sat Brigham Young.

He eyed Pogue with a steady gaze from eyes as cold and flat as pewter. It was difficult to discern his height while seated, but he appeared to Pogue to be average, perhaps slightly smaller, in stature. The Mormon prophet was portly, with sandy-colored hair going gray growing to a length that hung below his ears and over the collar. A beard fringed his jawline. The angle of his eyebrows, wrinkles at the corners of his eyes, furrowed forehead, and down-turned mouth suggested a humorless, sober man.

As if on cue, a door beside the rolltop desk opened, and a small man with an oversized bound book bustled into the room from elsewhere in the house and took a seat at the writing table. He opened the book, the pages of which were filled with hand-writing, and paged through to a blank page. From a writing set on the desk, he uncapped an inkwell, picked up a pen, and inserted a nib.

"State your business," Young said.

Pogue cleared his throat, disarmed by the interview's blunt

beginning. "I am Calvin Pogue, an operative of the Pinkerton—"

"I know all that," Young interrupted. "I am also aware that you are investigating the shooting of Lilburn Boggs with the intent of hanging it on Porter Rockwell. What do you want of me?"

Again, the man's directness rattled the detective.

"May I sit?" Pogue asked in a bid to buy time and composure.

"I suppose. But don't get too comfortable. Your time here will be short, if I'm not mistaken."

Pogue lowered himself into one of two straight-backed, wooden chairs with upholstered seats sitting in the corner of the room opposite Young's desk and then lifted his stiff knee with both hands as he rotated slightly to face his host.

"How did you come to be a cripple, Mr. Pogue?"

"The war. Combat wound. Rifle ball removed a good part of my knee, mangled the rest beyond repair."

"That war seems to have created much damage. To the nation and to people like you. Which side?"

"I fought for the Union, sir." Pogue studied the man for a moment and then asked, "You?"

"Excuse me?" Young said, taken aback by the question.

"Were you involved in the war out here in Utah, sir?"

Young licked his lips, considering his answer. "Not directly. I am an old man, as you see, and by the time the war started, the federal government had stripped me of any political office. We— the Mormon people—sent no troops to the war. We provided militia troops to protect the mails and the Overland Trail early on, but our duties there were usurped by the California Volunteers. Sent here, primarily, to keep an eye on me."

"Sir?"

"We are a law-abiding people, Mr. Pogue. Strong for the Constitution. Both parties to that infernal war trampled on that document, and I could not, in good conscience, offer either faction my firm support. Had they destroyed one another I would not have mourned.

"Had that been the case, we stood ready to uphold the Constitution, pick up the pieces, and rebuild the nation as God intended, according to constitutional principles."

Pogue absorbed the prophet's statement, listening, as he did, to the scratch of pen across paper as the third man in the room, barely noticeable were it not for the quiet noise of his writing, recorded the conversation—for what purpose, the detective could not imagine.

"I seem to recall that your man Rockwell served with the army."

"As a civilian contractor. He was hired on as a scout and guide for Colonel Connor's bloody foray against the Shoshoni on the Bear River in Cache Valley. He was reluctant in service, but I advised him to comply with Connor's wishes. I was equally reluctant to offer such counsel but figured it would serve the greater good to maintain a cooperative, if not cordial, relationship with the army."

"Rockwell obeyed your wishes, despite misgivings?"

Young eyed his inquisitor cautiously. "He did. Port is, above all else, loyal. He is true blue to the Church and unhesitant in carrying out the will and wishes of those in its leadership. It was so during Joseph's time and has remained so since.

"Because of that loyalty, he performed his assignment with the troops with distinction. Even earned the respect of Colonel Connor and his troops. Matter of fact, he became cozier with the colonel—he was promoted to general after Bear River; you must excuse my habitual reference to his lower rank—than I approved.

"But Port, while loyal, is also independent and goes his own way. We allow that so long as it does not interfere with our work. His relationship with Connor, while distasteful to me personally, seems harmless enough. Port would never do anything to compromise the Church, and I take comfort in that."

Pogue removed the notebook and pencil from the pocket of his suit coat and asked if Young objected to his taking notes. He folded back the cover and the filled pages, made a brief notation on a clean page, and asked, "Apparently loyalty isn't Rockwell's only quality. I have been told by many that he is a capable and resourceful man."

"You have been correctly informed. There is no man I know of or have heard of more attuned to life on the frontier than Port. I fear, now that this is primarily a civilized nation from coast to coast, that his abilities are less in demand and, in fact, of little use. But his day is not yet past, and I am confident he will continue to ply his skills as needed."

"Would you expand on those skills?"

"Where to begin? Much of Port's time nowadays is occupied recovering stolen stock. Cattle, horses, mules, oxen, sheep—the man is tenacious in his recovery efforts and will not give up until he has returned the animals to their rightful owner. As God is my witness, Port could track yesterday's songbird's flight across an empty sky. Where others lose a trail, he will find it. Sometimes I think he has second sight. Could be he smells it on the wind. Maybe he just reasons out where to go. Whatever it is, Port can find and follow a track where no other man can.

"He is also a remarkable man with a horse. I particularly admire that in him, as my relationship with horses has always been a tenuous one. But, riding or driving, Port can get more speed and more miles out of a horse than anyone. Without harm to the animal, I might add. He can gentle and train the roughest horses.

"Port also knows cattle and can manage a herd with outstanding economy. He has made a good deal of money over the years buying, selling, and trading stock. Had he the same ability to control his finances, Port would be a wealthy man."

Pogue asked about other assignments Rockwell had fulfilled. Young said he had made countless trips back and forth across the plains in service to the Church. Guiding wagon trains of settlers, escorting Church leaders on official business, running freight trains with supplies, carrying the mail and other correspondence—the list spilled out faster than Pogue could write it down.

The Mormon president touched lightly on Rockwell's service in the church militia during the Utah War, and Pogue asked for details.

"No, I see no need to expand on that unfortunate time. Suffice it to say that Port played his part in keeping the invading troops at bay, allowing us time to work out a peaceful resolution. He did as asked. Port, and a few other hardy souls, stood off the entire United States Army, brought it to its knees without shedding a drop of blood.

"I assure you, had the occasion called for it, our boys would have driven the army across lots in order to protect this people. As it was, it only required burning a few wagonloads of supplies and driving off a herd of government cattle."

"I am also told Rockwell is a gunman of some talent."

"For a fact. He is a crack shot, pistol or rifle, and is seldom second best in a target shooting competition."

"How about in shooting scrapes with men?"

Young carefully considered his reply. "Clearly, Port has yet to come out second best in those unfortunate incidents. His cool head, sharp eye, and steady hand have served him—and the cause of law and order—well."

"Your contention is that all the shootings and killings attributed to him have been in service to the law?"

"Absolutely."

"Let me ask about his hair and beard. Do you put any credence in Joseph Smith's 'prophecy' or whatever it may be called that so long as he did not cut his hair, he would be protected from harm?"

"Absolutely. The proof is in the man, in that he is still among us. Port has walked away miraculously unharmed on many, many occasions.

"Still, you have it wrong, Mr. Pogue. Port's untrimmed hair and beard get all the notice, but that is only half the story. Joseph's prophecy—which is certainly what it was, make no mistake—is also contingent on Port's loyalty. Joseph's invocation of heavenly protection requires that Port 'remain true to the faith.' I have no doubt—no doubt—that if Port fulfills his end, the Lord will shield him and he will die peacefully in his bed, an old man."

Pogue and Young's scribe wrote in silence for a few moments.

"I appreciate your time and information, Mr.—President Young. I hope, finally, you will tell me what you know of the shooting of Lilburn Boggs."

"I know nothing of it, Mr. Pogue, except that it happened. I was otherwise occupied at the time and nowhere near Jackson County."

"What is—was—your opinion of Governor Boggs?"

"No man ever lived who is as evil. He thwarted the work of the Lord repeatedly. His actions caused the blood of the Saints to be murderously shed on many occasions. He persecuted our people, stole our property and possessions, drove us from our Zion. He allowed—caused—widows and orphans to starve. He was relentless in his mistreatment of us, even after we left his pestiferous state. Why, even as he preceded us west, he attempted to poison the waters, speaking ill of us at every opportunity to turn people against us."

"Those opinions are, as I understand, widely held among your people. Surely you can understand why suspicion would fall on the Mormons concerning the assassination attempt on the governor."

"Perhaps," Young said. "But this people is content to allow the Lord to exact punishment on those who persecute us. And we do not doubt that he does and will. I testify to you here and now that God is, even as we speak, taking his vengeance against Lilburn Boggs. Without doubt or contradiction, it is pretty hot for the governor right now."

"You must have some ideas or opinions about who shot him."

"I do. But they are just that—opinions. They have no basis in fact any more than the accusations made against Port."

"So what are they? Your opinions, I mean."

Again, Young sat silent, his steadfast gaze discomfiting Pogue as he formulated a response.

"Governor Boggs was a politician. He was not well liked and had many rivals—enemies, even. His fiscal policies as governor were unwise and unpopular. Even his persecution of the Saints was detested by many in the state. It could be that one of his political opponents wanted him eliminated. No doubt his many years in trade made enemies, as well, as often happens in business. Someone he wronged in commerce may have sought revenge.

"It seems, as well, if memory serves, that another man was blamed for the shooting, even before Port. But, as I said, I do not know who shot Governor Boggs, nor why. Nor do I particularly care."

"A former colleague of yours, John Bennett, said he believed— knew—Rockwell was guilty of the crime and that he acted on orders from Joseph Smith."

"Another liar. John C. Bennett is the spawn of Satan. That man nearly destroyed this church with his lies. He spread evil throughout Nauvoo and blamed Joseph for it. When exposed as a fraud and hypocrite, he sought revenge with his sharp tongue and wicked pen. Not one word he ever spoke or wrote can be accepted as truth. His lying ways are clearly revealed in the records.

"Just as it is the unchangeable nature of a rattlesnake to strike, a liar will always lie. Thus, the contemptible Bennett."

Pogue closed his notebook and returned it with the pencil to his pocket. The secretary continued his entries in his bound journal. The detective thanked his host as he rose to leave, asking a final question as he shook hands with the reputed most powerful man in western America.

"So it is your firm opinion, then, that Porter Rockwell did not shoot Governor Boggs."

"No, it is not my opinion, Mr. Pogue. It is a certainty—if only, for no other reason, that Boggs survived. Had Port fired the shot, that would not have been the case."

———◆———

When I got home from California in '48, which would have been about June, the folks in charge figured Brigham ought to be well on the way with another company of Saints and that I ought to go meet up with them and help them on to Salt Lake, which I did.

After no more'n a day or two in town, I saddled up and rode east. Just shy of Scott's Bluff I found them, comin' along just fine. I did some huntin' for them, made certain they stayed to the best part of the trail, and scouted out places for the people to lay over and graze for the stock.

Led that party into the valley late in September.

That time I got to stay awhile and spent the winter herdin' cattle all up and down the Salt Lake Valley and elsewhere, trying to keep them in enough grass. It was a job, I'll tell you. I put a lot of miles on a lot of mounts huntin' graze down in Utah Valley, out west to Cedar Valley and Rush Valley too. There was too much snow and not enough grass, and it was a rough winter on them cattle.

Another thing that happened along about that time, leastways come the spring, was that I was named a deputy marshal for the State of Deseret. That was what we called it then, see, not being a part of the United States nor wantin' to be. We was makin' our own country. Later on, when the Mexican war was settled, the USA convinced us our land had been won by them from Mexico and we was part of their sorry country. They made us into Utah Territory, and I become a deputy United States marshal, which I was ever after and am still, I suppose.

I pass that along in case you're inclined to believe any of them tales about my bein' an outlaw. Far from it. I'm a lawman, see, and have been since '49.

Along about that same time, that spring, I was told to hit the road again. Back to California.

This time, I'd be headin' right into that part of the country where Lilburn Boggs was in charge. I didn't relish the thought, I'll tell you. I knowed from experience that he wasn't above settin' the dogs on me—be they bounty hunters, lawmen, mobbers, or whatever manner of man he had at hand. And I figured he'd find a lot better men than them Missouri pukes he'd set on me before, what with him bein' in charge of a sizeable chunk of California, and the place already crawlin' with gold hunters.

I figured I could hold my own with any man that come to get me—long as I could see him comin'. And never bein' in that part of the country before, I wasn't sure where to look for trouble.

The reason we was goin' to California, though, wasn't nothin' to do with Boggs. I didn't want no trouble with that man, nor did any Mormon, so far as I knew.

No, we was goin' to California huntin' one of our own—Sam Brannan, whose name you might've heard me mention before.

THIRTY-TWO

POGUE WENT FROM the Beehive House and his meeting with Brigham Young to a small main street café and then returned to the Salt Lake House. Along with his room key, the desk clerk passed him a letter.

THE CHURCH OF JESUS CHRIST
OF LATTER-DAY SAINTS
OFFICE OF THE PRESIDENT
SALT LAKE CITY, UTAH TERRITORY

Calvin Pogue
c/o Salt Lake House Hotel

Mr. Pogue:

Pursuant to our conversation just completed, I have determined not to object to your continued presence in the city or territory. While I find the nature of your business distasteful, it is also, I believe, inconsequential.

Because others may not be as accepting of your work here, I would encourage you to complete your business promptly and not linger any longer than prudent. The city police have been informed and will endeavor to ensure your safety.

> *Very respectfully yours,*
> *s/Brigham Young*

———————◆———————

Our plan once we got to California was to just lay low, get the lay of the land, and figure out what Sam Brannan was up to.

See, he was in New York or somewheres when the move west started, so Brigham Young assigned him to see our folks in that country got moved. He arranged for a ship and sailed for California and got settled in at San Francisco before the rest of us even got started.

He rode east and met Brigham Young in Salt Lake not long after we got there, sayin' the Saints ought to keep right on goin' and settle in California. But Brigham, he was determined on stayin' where he was, figurin' if California was the garden spot Brannan claimed it was, plenty of other folks would be wantin' to go there. He was content to be in a place unlikely to attract a lot of neighbors—what with our experience amongst neighbors not bein' all that good.

Well, that didn't set too well with Brannan, so he went back to San Francisco thinkin' Brigham was a fool.

It got sort of touchy after that, as part of Brannan's work in the Church was actin' as leader of them in California, gettin' everybody all situated there and helpin' one another and collectin' the tithing and such. Thing was, not one penny of that tithing money made it to Salt Lake. And Brigham knew Brannan had it, on account of reports from Battalion boys that drifted home from time to time.

Amasa Lyman—he was the man Brigham sent to deal with Brannan—hung around Sutter's Fort, where Brannan was getting' rich runnin' a store, and in San Francisco seein' what all the man had his fingers into and what he was doin' with that Church money.

Me, I headed into the mountains and the diggin's, figurin' to pan out a small fortune—not bein' the greedy sort, a small one would've been fine. By then—this would've been early in the summer of '49—them mountains was already crawlin' with gold hunters, and I soon enough seen that wadin' around in them cold rivers wasn't for me.

So I sold off my outfit and went partners on a saloon at Murderer's

Bar. I say saloon, but it weren't nothin' more than a round tent with rough furnishings and watered-down whiskey. I took the name of Brown, Jim Brown, on account of there bein' a fair amount of Missouri pukes and Illinois rowdies there in the gold fields, and it's likely some might have been upset at the sound of my name.

Besides, I was in Boggs's country and saw no need to announce to him my bein' there.

Anyways, my partner mostly kept bar, and I spent most of my time in the saddle, haulin' pack trains of whiskey in from Sutter's Fort. I don't mind sayin' I was careful about it—it bein' dangerous work on its own and me bein' a likely target for any number of ne'er-do-wells, Boggs's men or others, should they know who I was.

I kept a rifle on my saddle at all times and a pair of capped-and-loaded revolvers in my pockets or belt. I even had a couple of old duelin' pistols packed full of buck and ball. They'd have probably blowed up in my face had I ever occasion to pull the trigger on them!

Best thing, though, was this little white dog I had back then. Trained him to ride behind my saddle, so he was always on the look-out. Trained him too to lick my face quiet-like if we were in camp or sleepin' when strangers was a-comin'. That way, see, he didn't set up a howlin' and barkin', which would've let them know I knew they were there. No sir, I wanted them to think they was gettin' the drop on me without knowin' I had the drop on them.

Well, that went on for a time and then by and by—dead of winter, would've been January of '50—Amasa Lyman decided it was time to pay Sam Brannan a call.

We found him in San Francisco. He was a big man there, maybe the richest man in town, what with all the gold he'd taken in trade from the miners at his store at Sutter's and in San Francisco. What money he'd taken in tithing from them California Saints didn't hurt any either.

Brannan, he didn't know me, only by name. I guess he'd heard I wasn't no man to mess with, for he was plenty enough nervous. Still, he was all bluff and bluster and pretty much told Amasa he could go to the devil, and Brigham Young too. When Lyman said that money weren't his but the Lord's, Brannan just puffed up and says "Yer right, Brother Lyman. And soon as you hand over a receipt signed by the Lord, I'll hand over the money."

That was the end of Sam Brannan so far as the Mormons was concerned. After that, he made it known he wanted no part of the Church no more, and the Church sure wanted no part of him.

Found out later him and Boggs was friends, even then.

THIRTY-THREE

THE CARRIAGE HIRED to take Pogue to Fort Douglas, some three miles uphill to the east from downtown, first took a short detour to the Colorado Stables. Among Porter Rockwell's several enterprises, the stable bought, sold, rented, and boarded horses and mules, many bearing his famous OP brand.

The detective did not expect to find Rockwell on the premises. Word was, he spent most of his time at his ranch on Government Creek out on the west desert or through the Jordan River gap at a home in the town of Lehi. Pogue would leave word, however, requesting a meeting.

"Yes, you can leave a note for Port. I'll see he gets it should he happen by," the hostler said. "Thing is, it won't do you a bit of good."

"Why's that?"

"The man can't read. Not a word. Can't write, neither."

"You?"

"I can get by. Better with sums than letters though."

"If I leave this with you, will you read it to Mr. Rockwell and inform him of my wish to meet?"

"Sure. Let's have a look."

Tipping his hat back, the stable man looked down his nose at the note paper, adjusting it back and forth to find his focus. Pogue watched his mouth move as he deciphered the words.

"So, you're a Pinkerton man. Say your name."

"Pogue, Calvin Pogue."

"Right. As I read this, you want Port to call on you at the Salt Lake House whenever it's handy, and if you're not there leave word when and where you can find him."

"That's correct," the detective said, handing the man a dollar. "Thank you, and please take this for your trouble."

"Oh, that ain't necessary, Mr. Pogue."

"Certainly not—but I insist."

———◆———

Fort Douglas, formerly Camp Douglas, had been established by Colonel Patrick Edward Connor immediately upon his arrival in the Salt Lake Valley late in 1862 to house the infantry and cavalry troops of the California Volunteers under his command. The troops, mustered in California and trained in the early days of the Civil War, hoped to go east to fight the rebels.

Instead, they were assigned to the desolation of the Great Basin to protect the Overland Trail and transcontinental telegraph line to eliminate the chance of California being cut off and to protect emigrants venturing west against Indian troubles.

Connor saw it his duty, as well, to discipline the disloyal Mormons, if necessary. In seeking approval for the establishment of the camp after an exploratory visit to the city, he wrote this to his superiors: "I found them a community of traitors, murderers, fanatics, and whores. . . . The people publicly rejoice at reverses to our arms, and thank God that the American government is gone, as they term it. . . .

". . . I intend to quietly intrench my position, and then say to the Saints of Utah, enough of your treason."

And so he established his camp on the benchland above the city and, to further insult the Mormons, named it after one of their Illinois enemies, Stephen A. Douglas.

But Connor was not allowed to make war on the Latter-day

Saints and, since there were no confederates to fight, set his sights on the Indians. Within months of his arrival in the territory, he launched a sneak attack on a Shoshoni village on the banks of the Bear River in Cache Valley, slaughtering some three hundred men, women, and children.

The expedition, undertaken in the dead of winter, was the colonel's introduction to Porter Rockwell. Despite personal mis-givings about trusting a Mormon, Connor was assured that no man alive could serve his purposes as guide and scout as well as Rockwell.

If the arduous expedition was a test between the two men, they passed. Each learned a grudging respect for the other. And, despite the soldier's undying hatred of the Mormons and the frontiers-man's eternal hatred of the army, they became friends.

Connor, promoted to Brigadier General for his Bear River exploits, mustered out of the army in 1866 but maintained a home in Utah Territory and spent much of his time there, looking after mining interests. Even as an army officer, he encouraged his sol-diers and anyone else he could convince to prospect for and mine the minerals concealed in the mountains, believing an influx of outsiders spurred by mining would dilute and then overwhelm Mormon influence.

And he pursued mineral riches himself. Beyond the Oquirrh Mountains west of Salt Lake Valley, he built a mill, a smelter, and the town of Stockton to process ore extracted from his claims.

Pogue knew the retired general maintained close ties with the officers at Fort Douglas, and the investigator hoped to learn from them his whereabouts. The adjutant Pogue encountered at head-quarters at Fort Douglas knew and had served under Connor.

"He was a great soldier, the general. Fearless and dedi-cated. He was firm with his men. Demanded the best of them. Brooked no weakness or lack of discipline. 'Twas a pleasure to serve under him."

"How long have you known him?"

"Not ten years. Met him in California when he organized the Stockton Blues."

"Stockton Blues?"

"Militia unit. General Connor was a military man in his heart, so he made an army of his own. He'd had to give up his commission, you know."

But Pogue did not know. The adjutant proclaimed Connor a military hero, wounded at the Battle of Buena Vista in the Mexican War, where he was captain of a company of Texas Volunteers. His wound forced him from the army, and he went to California.

But when Civil War threatened, Connor again offered his service, was commissioned a colonel, and brought the California Volunteers to Utah Territory. Promoted to Brigadier General and later put in command of the entire District of the Plains, he had been military chief over vast regions of the western mountains and plains.

"He's been back and forth between the Stocktons since his discharge," the adjutant laughed. "Stockton in California and his own Stockton out west by Rush Valley, that is.

"You're in luck if you're looking for him, for he's here now. In town, I mean. I know that, on account of the Connors haven't a house here in the city anymore. So when he's in town without the Mrs., he bunks here in the officer's quarters, as he did last night. You might find him at the Wells Fargo freight office. Said he had to arrange some shipments of mining equipment."

Pogue hurried the hired carriage downhill and along the length of Brigham Street, thinking himself fortunate. With luck, he might be able to interview Patrick Connor without leaving the city.

He hoped to be as lucky in locating Porter Rockwell.

◆

After that business with Sam Brannan, I figured if Boggs didn't already know I was in California, he would soon enough find out. But there wasn't nothing to be done about it that I wasn't already doin', so I kept my eyes open and my guns loaded and capped.

And things went on as usual. Amasa Lyman stayed around there until August—this was still 1850—tryin' to work some angle to settle up with Brannan but finally gave it up and decided to go on home. I got him safe through the mountains and then went back to Murderer's Bar and Mormon Tavern. Business was good there, and so far as I knew I had no better prospects in Salt Lake.

Not long after I got back there, one of our Battalion boys, loud-mouth feller name of Stewart, got on a toot and thought to challenge me to a shootin' contest. Now Stewart, see, he'd been makin' out pretty good with a tradin' post thereabouts and had him a nice pile of gold. Him bein' a braggart and a troublemaker besides, he figured he'd add to it with a wager.

I told him go to the devil at first, me not wantin' to be noticed and all. But he kept at me, and when he wagered a thousand dollars in gold that he could outshoot me in a target contest, well, I decided why not.

Word got around about the match between Stewart and "Brown," and there was hundreds of men showed up for it. That gold country was lackin' in amusements at the time, see, and them miners would fall out for nearly any commotion.

Stewart wasn't no slouch with a gun, but the fact is there ain't many a man can shoot better'n me. 'Fore long I had me a nice little poke full of dust and nuggets for my trouble.

Turned out to be more trouble than it was worth.

With all them men gathered and all that excitement and all that money floatin' around—see, my thousand dollar prize wasn't but a smidgen of the gold that changed hands that day, what with hundreds of side bets made—someone would buy a drink for everyone in sight, then someone else'd return the favor, and whiskey started showin' up from every direction, and before you know it, we had the biggest drunken fandango ever seen in them parts. There was singin' and dancin' and fistfights all around in that tavern tent and spillin' out into the yard and all about. High times, I'll tell you.

Stewart, though, he weren't none too happy. Should've known he'd be a sore loser.

Anyways, he got pretty liquored up after a while and was gettin' madder with every dram. Next thing you know, he's a-standin' atop a

whiskey barrel—and barely able to do it, weavin' about as he was—
and hollerin' out for the attention of the crowd. Finally, he fires a shot
skyward, which quietened things down right quick.

"Do you know who I am?" he yelled, wobblin' up there and
wavin' his pistol about. "Sure you do. I'm Boyd Stewart! I'm the man
who was beat in this shootin' match here today!"

That brought up a cheer from the crowd, but Stewart kept wavin'
his arms about to shush 'em up.

"What I bet you don't know," he hollered, "is the name of the
man that bested me!"

That triggered another round of shouts and cheers and such, and
men raisin' their glasses and toastin' "Brown! Brown! Brown!"

But Stewart snapped off another cap to hush 'em up, which
started me into worryin' on account of Stewart, see, he knew who I
was from way back.

"No!" he yelled. "He ain't no Brown! Not by a long shot! That
man, that one who calls hisself Brown—that's Porter Rockwell!"

Well, there weren't a breath took in that place for what seemed
a good long time. Them few as knew me were surprised, I suspect, to
see me revealed.

Them that only knowed my name was too, I suppose, for other
reasons. See, I had something of a reputation as a gunman, even
then—especially around Missouri and Illinois, where plenty of them
gold hunters had come from.

Well, before you know it, them pukes started formin' up into
a lynch mob, with me bein' their object. It was nip and tuck there
for a bit, but I fought 'em off long enough—with the help of some
of the Battalion boys and other Mormons that was there—to slice
through that tent wall with my knife and slip off into the woods.
I hid out till they tired of lookin' for me, which didn't take long,
what with most all them boys bein' so drunk they could barely stay
upright.

A few days later, a party of men was wantin' to go back to Salt
Lake, so I jumped at the chance to guide them. I figured things'd
be too hot for me in the goldfields from then on, what with them
Missouri pukes and other Mormon haters knowin' who I was. And,

truth be told, I's still some worried about Boggs sendin' assassins after me. God knows there wouldn't have been no shortage of volunteers for the job.

Anyways, I got back to Salt Lake after bein' more'n a year and a half in them gold fields. And, so far as I know, I never again got within five hundred miles of Lilburn Boggs.

THIRTY-FOUR

PATRICK EDWARD CONNOR was, indeed, at the Wells Fargo office when the detective arrived. A clerk in the outer office confirmed the fact and identified which of the raised voices heard from an interior office belonged to the general. Gold leaf lettering on the pebbled-glass window in the door identified the office as belonging to the manager. And while the walls muffled the voices so as to make overhearing the conversation impossible, there was no doubt it was heated.

Selecting a week-old *Chicago Tribune* from a pile of newspapers spread on a table, Pogue settled in to wait for Connor to complete his business. Absorbed in the news of his hometown, he almost missed the general when the manager's office door burst open and a man rushed through the reception area and out the front door.

"That," the clerk said, "was your General Connor."

Tossing the newspaper onto the table, Pogue hurried after him in time to see Connor round the corner of the building. He hobbled along the sidewalk as fast as his stiffened leg would allow. He saw the general climb into a hack.

"General Connor! General Connor!"

Connor looked irritated at the interruption but signaled the driver to stop.

Pogue approached the buggy. "Thank you for waiting."

As the man inside studied him, Pogue noted the General's Irish-red hair was streaked with gray, as were his muttonchop whiskers and moustache. His face appeared windburned or sunburned and had begun to wrinkle like boot leather.

"I hoped to catch you in the freight office, but you left too quickly."

Connor snorted. "Wells Fargo fools. They've got all but a monopoly on shipping around here and so they squeeze a man for every penny. But that's not your problem. Who are you, and what is?"

Pogue presented the credentials that identified him as an operative of the Pinkerton Detective Agency and asked if he could speak with the general concerning a case.

"I've lots to do. How much time will you require?"

"Not long. But I will need your attention. Could you, perhaps, join me for lunch? Even the busiest man must take time to eat."

"Get in."

Connor directed the driver to a favorite eatery. Along the way, he quizzed Pogue on his injured leg. Interested in the details of his service, the general peppered the investigator with questions about where he had served and who his superior officers were. He expressed disappointment at not being in the thick of the late war, instead serving at a post in the remote West, where opportunities to fight were limited.

Of especial disappointment, he said, was not being allowed to whip the treasonous Mormons into submission. Even now, he wished he could take up arms against the curious sect and forever eliminate their power and influence in the West.

The conversation spilled over into the café and halfway through the meal. Finally, Connor said, "I'm sorry. I'm taking up your time with my harangue. Blame it on my Irish. What is it you wished to speak with me about?"

"A man I believe to be of your acquaintance. Orrin Porter Rockwell."

"Ah, yes. Porter. As fine a man as ever I've met. A bit rough

around the edges but a real man through and through. An officer with a hundred men like him in his command could whip
an army. Ah, but I doubt there's a dozen like him, let alone a
hundred."

Pogue asked his history with the Mormon gunman. "I've
heard some of it in the course of my inquiries but would like to
hear it from you."

"I knew of Rockwell long before I came to Utah Territory.
He was something of a legend in the Gold Country. Almost as
if he wasn't real but more like an invention meant to frighten.
Like with Joaquin Murrieta, you see—someone to blame for every
wrongdoing. Yes, Porter was well known, even then. Known and
talked of most everywhere in the West.

"He was the last man I wanted to employ, but when we
endeavored to punish the Shoshoni and I needed a reliable guide
to take us to the savages, I was told repeatedly that Rockwell was
the best choice for that kind of work.

"Which turned out to be true. Had we not had him with us,
we'd have never convinced the traitorous Cache Valley Mormons
to point out the precise location of the Indian camp on the Bear
River, and the murderous heathens might have skated.

"After the fight, he rounded up teams and drivers and sleighs
and wagons to haul our dead and wounded and captured goods
off the battlefield and out of the valley. Without Porter's influence,
I do not doubt those Mormons would have left us to freeze and
die on that godforsaken river bottom.

"We became fast friends then. Me and a Mormon, if you can
imagine. I used his services afterward when occasion demanded
and came to trust him without question. I'd trust Porter with my
very life, and that of my family. And I'll not say such of many
men."

Pogue wondered if there was any truth to reports that Rockwell committed murder and other atrocities on orders from his
Church leaders.

"Sure there is. He's told me so himself. See, Porter and I share
a liking for a drink from time to time, and when in our cups, we

often trade stories. We've spent many a pleasant hour talking and emptying a whiskey bottle. I say pleasant—but some of the things he told me in those hours could shrivel your manhood.

"Much of what he told me is common knowledge, some whispered rumors, other things hidden so deep they will never see light. No matter. So long as he remains in Utah Territory or under the protection of the Mormons, he need not fear. It is a sad fact that the law could not touch Joseph Smith, nor can it touch Brigham Young. The Mormons have the courts here bought and paid for and can rent out who and what they don't own. They've never been called to account for their evil doings and heinous crimes and likely never will."

"What about Rockwell's role in it all? Do you think he should answer for it?"

Connor considered the question for a moment.

"I'm a military man, Mr. Pogue. I guess the best answer I can give is that Porter is a good soldier. Loyal. Trusted. He was only following orders."

"Did he ever talk about his days in Missouri? In particular, the shooting of Governor Boggs there?"

"He did. 'I shot through the window,' said he during our merrymaking one time, 'and I thought I had killed him, but I had only wounded him. I was sorry that I had not killed the man.' That's how he put it."

Pogue completed his notes, thanked the general, and returned to the Salt Lake House. He stopped at the desk to retrieve his room key, and the clerk said Porter Rockwell was waiting for him in the public room.

◆

CASE NOTES OF CALVIN POGUE

"That's about the size of it, so far as me and Lilburn Boggs goes."

Rockwell poured us another "squar" whiskey—the last of how

many, I can't say. And while I moderated my intake as much as possible and confined my drinks to whiskey, he drank freely of the liquor and added a considerable amount of beer to the mix. The boozing seemed to have no effect on the man. Since that visit was the one and only time I ever saw him, I can honestly report that I don't know if I never saw him drunk or never saw him sober.

He hoisted his glass, as usual, with a call of "Wheat!" and poured off the drink. Then he talked on.

"When word came down Boggs died—for certain this time—there was plenty of celebratin' goin' on amongst the Mormons. Can't think there'll ever be another man for us to hate as much as he was hated. Maybe them that killed Joseph, but they was cowardly mobbers that no one could identify for sure. Other than Frank Worrell, and I got him, but good."

All the while during my one-sided conversation with Rockwell, the beer bucket on the table had been replenished regularly and the whiskey bottle, when empty, had been replaced by a full one.

As he talked and drank and talked, he had kept his hands busy, reducing the size of a pine block with his pocket knife. Curled shavings had slowly fallen away from the shapeless block to reveal a most remarkable carving of a horse.

He handed me the hunk of pine, said it was mine to keep if I wanted it.

I wanted it. I knew just where it belonged.

I turned and twisted and admired it at every angle. It should not have surprised me that a man legendary for his affinity with the horse should understand so intimately its appearance. But the delicate artistry with which this crude frontiersman depicted the animal was truly shocking.

The carving—sculpture, if you will—was of the portion of the horse we would call, in a man, a bust.

The stallion's head was tucked back tight against an arched, heavily muscled neck. Rockwell had somehow captured the horse's strength, grace, and power as it fought the bit in its teeth, so the motion in the piece was all forward, despite carefully carved taut reins drawing the muzzle backward. Flared nostrils, flowing mane, and rippled muscles accentuated the struggle toward freedom, the fight against restraint.

"Boggs, now, he didn't hide behind nothin' nor nobody. Threatened to kill every last one of us, he did. Stood up on his hind legs and shouted out his disgust for Mormons for all to hear.

"Got to give him that, I suppose.

"Now, I know there's plenty who say I shot Boggs that time in Missouri. Never mind that a jury of them pukes couldn't pin it on me.

"That's why you're here, I suppose, to see if I'll own up to it. I'll say this, and nothing more.

"I never killed that man.

"And if ever I'd had the chance, I'd have done it again."

THIRTY-FIVE

THE NIGHT HAD BEEN a long one, but dawn was yet to pale the sky when Pogue climbed, somewhat unsteadily, to his upstairs room at the Salt Lake House, leaving Rockwell propped against the wall in his wooden chair tossing back a long drink of whiskey and chasing it with a flood of beer. Although tired, the Pinkerton man took the time to review his notes from the conversation, adding detail and expanding his entries with the gunman's comments still fresh in his weary mind.

Finding a second wind in the work, Pogue located a few sheets of hotel stationery in a drawer, scratched out a note, wrote a letter, and drafted a telegram. With the day now well underway and his work blotted and dry, he rubbed the wrinkles from his face and jacket front and set out into the city to ship a parcel, post the letter, and wire the telegram.

A peek into the common room on the way out of the hotel showed Rockwell gone, but the flotsam and jetsam of their long conversation still littered the area—a beer bucket crusted with dried foam, a couple of empty whiskey bottles and filmy glasses on the table, and a scattering of wood shavings on the carpeted floor surrounding Rockwell's erstwhile seat.

First to the post office, where a clerk helped Pogue find a suitable box for the whittled horsehead, inserted the note for Emily

Elizabeth, and filled the gaps with crumpled paper. The clerk calculated postage for the parcel and Pogue's letter, accepted payment, and tossed the pieces onto a stack of outgoing mail.

Then to the Western Union office, where a persnickety clerk read and reread his telegram to the home office and relieved Pogue's pocket of the price of delivery.

With no appetite for breakfast—or lunch—it was again to the Salt Lake House, where the investigator intended to collapse into his bed for as long as possible and then catch the first eastbound stage available, connect up with the railroad somewhere on the plains, and settle in for Chicago and what he hoped would be a lengthy stay.

THIRTY-SIX

Emily Elizabeth, my darling—

Soon after this beautiful stallion finds a home in your stables, I will be home myself. Having been away from you so long—too long—it is my hope to stay close to you. I will seek work, whether with Mr. Pinkerton or elsewhere, that allows me to stay in Chicago with you and your mother. Our family has been too long apart, and I hope to remedy that. Watch for me, and I hope you await my arrival with the same eagerness I feel.

Until then,
Father

———◆———

Salt Lake City, Utah Territory

William M. Boggs
Napa, Calif.

Dear Bill,

I believe I have, at this juncture, pursued every possible avenue of investigation into the shooting of your father in

Independence, Missouri, on May 6, 1842.

Since more than twenty-five years have passed since the unfortunate event, most, if not all, direct evidence in the case has long since ceased to exist. According to every source I have had the opportunity to exploit, there was little evidence to begin with, making inquiries at this late date almost insurmountably difficult.

I have attempted, somewhat, to keep you apprised of my activities throughout the investigation, so you are aware of the breadth of my inquiries. Every lead discovered has been followed. Every promising avenue explored. My exhaustive research and interviews in California, Illinois, Missouri, and Utah convince me that all that can be known is now known, and any further pursuit of information at this point would prove redundant, unfruitful, or both.

So, it is with some misgiving that I am constrained to report that I know little more of the facts of the case today than on the day last summer when we first met.

While I have immersed myself in the available information and developed opinions concerning the reliability and credibility of the various reports, as well as the people with knowledge of relevant events, I must emphasize that my opinions, while defensible and not without justification, are just that—opinions.

With that caution, allow me, please, to share my opinion on the matter, as derived from my investigation.

I am confident that Orrin Porter Rockwell is, indeed, the would-be assassin who fired the shot that wounded Lilburn W. Boggs and very nearly took his life. Among my reasons for arriving at this conclusion are

1. Rockwell's presence in the Independence area at the time is well known.
2. Rockwell was seen handling the murder weapon and is the last person known to have handled it before it was discovered missing from the store from which it was stolen.

3. *His rapid departure from that place immediately following the shooting is suspicious, as it is too opportune to be considered coincidental.*

4. *While some publicly accused a man named Tompkins shortly after the shooting, the county sheriff investigating the crime gave the accusation little credence.*

5. *As a Mormon, Rockwell's motive is obvious. The hatred members of that sect felt for Governor Boggs was well known, well documented, and publicly acknowledged.*

6. *Following his flight from Missouri, Rockwell's behavior further indicates guilt. Once the protection of the courts in Nauvoo appeared to weaken, he hid out for many months in the eastern states and only attempted to return to Nauvoo out of desperation.*

7. *While evidence—primarily from the late John C. Bennett, a disaffected Mormon—suggesting Joseph Smith ordered the killing and rewarded Rockwell for the attempt is unreliable, when Bennett confronted him with the accusation, Rockwell did not deny that he shot the governor, only that Smith ordered it. Other reports indicate that Rockwell never did deny committing the crime; his various prevarications do not constitute a firm denial.*

8. *Rockwell's reputation as a killer is well established. He has, beyond question, killed many men, and his tendency toward violence cannot be overlooked. This propensity to use gunplay has become even more evident in the intervening years.*

9. *General Patrick Edward Connor, whose veracity is beyond question, claims Rockwell admitted the shooting. However, the general says both he and Rockwell were intoxicated at the time, and the confession, given the nature of the conversation, may be interpreted as "swapping tales" so cannot be considered infallible. Connor told this to me directly and has told others the same.*

10. *When confronted about the attempted killing by this investigator, Rockwell, as is his wont, neither admitted nor denied it directly. Instead he beat around the bush with vague declarations.*

That, Mr. Boggs, is my best estimate of the situation. While I recognize it will be, in many ways, unsatisfactory to you and your family, I also believe the main question has been answered. While the evidence against Rockwell is circumstantial at best, there is not now nor has there ever been an alternative explanation of the crime that is as convincing.

So, while the evidence today, as it was then, would likely be insufficient to gain an indictment, let alone a conviction in a court of law—were it possible to bring a case at this late date—it is certainly damning.

Finally, to reiterate, it is my considered opinion and firm belief, based on my extensive investigations, that Orrin Porter Rockwell attempted to assassinate your father and, when he fled the scene, believed he had accomplished the foul deed.

If you have questions on specific points of the investigation, please do not hesitate to contact me, care of the Pinkerton Detective Agency office in Chicago. Until then,

I remain your humble and obedient servant,

s/Calvin Pogue

———◆———

WESTERN UNION TELEGRAPH COMPANY
SALT LAKE CITY, UTAH TERR.

ALLAN PINKERTON
PINKERTON NATIONAL DETECTIVE AGENCY
CHICAGO

HAVE COMPLETED BOGGS INVESTIGATION TO

BEST OF MY ABILITY

WILL PROVIDE COPY OF LETTER TO CLIENT REPORTING FINDINGS

AM RETURNING TO CHICAGO AND WILL BRIEF YOU FURTHER UPON ARRIVAL

URGENTLY REQUEST FUTURE ASSIGNMENTS CONFINED TO HOME OFFICE OWING TO FAMILY CIRCUMSTANCES

YOS &C &C CALVIN POGUE

THIRTY-SEVEN

THE ROOM WAS SO DARK it took Calvin Pogue a few moments to decide if he'd opened his eyes or not. He looked around and finally detected a rectangular patch of a slightly lighter shade of black and decided it must be a window. Another moment awakened a realization of where he was and why.

For as long as he could, the detective stayed still in the bed, rehashing the Boggs shooting before mentally closing the file. Then, for a time, he outlined in his mind the day and days to come. The prospect of a drawn-out, bone-jarring stagecoach ride across the Wasatch Mountains and Wyoming plains dampened his enthusiasm for rising, but the eventual arrival in Chicago and home blunted that apprehension.

When the confinement of sheets and blankets got the better of him, Pogue threw back the bedcovers. He sat up, swung his legs over the edge, found the floor, and sat for a moment kneading his eye sockets with the heels of his hands. He then raked fingernails through his hair, awakening the scalp with vigorous scratching.

A few tentative steps took him to where his trousers hung over the back of an upholstered chair. He stepped into one pants leg and then sat and slid the other over his stiff knee. Pogue thumbed the waistband button into its hole as he walked to the door, not bothering with the fly for the short trip down the hall. It would need unbuttoning when he reached the toilet anyway.

Daytime was a definite possibility by the time the detective returned to the room. He stared out the second-floor window at a dismal, dimly lit view of a flat-roofed building across a narrow alley and of the brick wall of a taller building beyond.

Pogue lit a lamp and rustled around the room, carefully arranging papers and notebooks before putting them in his valise, repacking his trunk, and stuffing most of what he'd need for the road into the carpetbag, saving out his shaving kit for last. He arranged his comb, shaving mug and brush, razor, and toothbrush atop a tall chest of drawers against the wall next to the window.

Holding his toothbrush over the washbowl on the small table beside the chest, he poured water from the pitcher to moisten the brush, dipped it in the tin of tooth powder, gave his teeth a good scrub, rinsed his mouth, and spit the water into the washbowl. Then he wiped his chin and slung the towel around his neck. He dumped the rinse water from the basin into the thunder mug and poured in fresh water for shaving.

He moistened the soap in the shaving mug, worked it into a foam, and brushed it onto his throat and cheeks. Bobbing and weaving before the hand mirror propped on the chest, he scraped away neck whiskers, dipping from time to time to rinse the blade of the straight razor in the washbowl. Pogue relieved one cheek of unwanted growth, carefully carving sharp edges to his mustache and Vandyke beard.

With one side complete, he turned his attention to the other.

The instant he tipped his head to apply the blade, window glass exploded and Pogue tipped over backward and hit the floor like an ax-felled slaughterhouse steer, the racket of his crash mingling with the still-echoing powder blast.

Within minutes, Pogue's hotel room door banged open and the desk clerk and a swamper rushed through. The detective heard none of it. He lay still and silent as a pool of viscous blood spread slowly on the hardwood floor, reflecting the sheen of soft morning light sifting through the shattered window.

"Oh my, oh my, oh my!" the desk clerk said, wringing his hands and shuffling his feet. "Go for the doctor!" he told the swamper. "And find the police!" he yelled, dropping to his knees next to the fallen detective.

Unsure what to do, he willed trembling hands to wrench the towel from under Pogue's neck and shoved a handful of the fabric into the bloody mess of the man's head. He swallowed back bile and stifled repeated gagging as the towel between his fingers turned wet and red.

After what seemed an eternity, a policeman rushed into the room. "What happened? Some old man stopped me on the street sayin' somebody'd been shot but ran for a doctor 'fore I could get any sense out of him. He did right, from the looks of it."

"Don't know what happened. We were downstairs. Heard a shot and something—him—hit the floor."

The policeman hitched up his pants and dropped to one knee next to the clerk. "Here, let me do that. Get more towels. And hot water. I'm guessing the doc will want it when he gets here."

Hurried footsteps receded down the hallway and returned. The clerk dumped a stack of towels and folded sheets into a heap on the floor and rushed away again. "I'll go to the kitchen for water," he said over his shoulder as he cleared the doorway.

By the time the doctor shuffled in, eyes sagging with sleep and spectacles so filmy the policeman wondered if he could see at all, the officer had discarded two hotel towels, so saturated with Pogue's blood as to be useless.

"Let's get him on the bed," the doctor said. Despite his age and corpulence, long experience handling bodies made the doctor's work appear effortless as he hoisted Pogue by the armpits and hefted him onto the bed with minimal assistance from the policeman's grasp of the detective's ankles.

As the doctor dealt with his unexpected patient, more police officers crowded into the room, clearing out the clot of curious chambermaids, kitchen workers, and hotel guests aroused by all the ruckus. When the assistant chief arrived, officers were swarming the room, and through the shattered window he saw two policemen slowly walking on the adjacent building, hands clasped behind their backs and eyes sweeping the roof. Another officer did the same in the alleyway below.

"Sergeant!" he called. "Fill me in."

"Well, sir, we don't know much yet. Before sunup, the night clerk heard a shot come through the window and this stranger hit the floor. Shot in the head, he is."

"Oh, he's no stranger. Leastways not to me. We had him in lockup just the other day. Suspicious acting, he was, so a night patrolman brought him in and held him for questioning. I questioned him. Turns out he's a Pinkerton man. Check his wallet, and you'll see his name is Calvin Pogue. Looking into the shooting of Governor Boggs way back when in Missouri, he was. Trying to hang it on Porter Rockwell, from what I gather."

"Must have upset someone."

"So it seems. In the head, you say?"

"Yes, sir. Bullet plowed a pretty deep furrow along the side," the sergeant said.

"Doc, what's the verdict?"

"He's still among the living, Chief. Lost a lot of blood, and he'll have a whale of a headache. Other than that, I suspect he'll be right as rain."

"Lucky man."

"That he is. Bullet knocked him colder than a wedge, but he's coming around."

And he was. Pogue heard voices. Muffled and distant, but growing nearer.

"Look here, sir," the sergeant said and crossed the room.

Pogue's eyes opened, slammed shut, and opened again. He squinted a few times to find focus and tipped his head gingerly toward the voices.

"Here's where the bullet went," the sergeant said.

There, nestled among the vines and flowers of the wallpaper, was a gouge and a black hole rimmed with blood and hair and small pieces of Pogue.

"Lead's still in there. Leastways, there's no hole in the hallway."

With the doctor's help, Pogue sat up on the edge of the bed as a police whistle sounded outside the window. The chief leaned out to see the policeman in the alley hold up a copper cartridge.

"It's fresh," he shouted. "Probably tossed off the roof. Henry—forty-four caliber rimfire."

"Not much help there," offered the sergeant. "Common enough round. Could be pistol or rifle, either one."

"True enough," the chief said. "You shed any light on this, Pogue?"

"Afraid not," Pogue said, wincing as the doctor wrapped—none too gently—rolled bandage around his head. "It was barely light outside. As you've probably gathered, I was standing there at that chest of drawers, shaving. If I hadn't tipped my head to have a go at my cheek when I did, I suspect that hole in the wall would be in the center of my forehead."

"Like as not."

The detective pulled on his shirt and tucked it into his trousers, strapped on his gun belt, and donned his vest.

"What's your game, Pogue? You act like you're going someplace."

"I am," he said as he pulled his suit coat sleeves up his arms. "I've got a stagecoach to catch." To the swamper, lurking in the background ever since fetching the doctor, he said, "Get my trunk to the station, if you will. Right away." He plopped his hat on his head, cringed, thought better of it, and stowed it in the carpetbag. Then he fetched the straight razor from the floor, swept the remains of his shaving gear into its kit, dropped it into the carpetbag atop the hat, and then snapped the jaws shut. "This too, please. I'll take the valise," he said as he picked it up and headed for the door.

"Hold up, Pogue!" the chief said. "We've got an investigation to conduct here. Aren't you interested in who did this?"

Pogue looked at him, closed the door, and walked away.

DISCUSSION QUESTIONS

1. The difficulties between Mormons and other Missouri citizens were not as simple or one-sided as often represented. What circumstances in the conflict led Governor Boggs to the extreme measure of issuing the infamous and unprecedented extermination order?

2. Most people with knowledge of the attempted assassination of Governor Boggs held definite opinions concerning the guilt or innocence of Porter Rockwell. Why do you suppose there was so much certainty and so little ambivalence about the crime?

3. Lilburn Boggs was an influential and important man on the western frontier. Why do you think he is remembered only for the extermination order among Mormons and virtually forgotten by everyone else?

4. Calvin Pogue's relationship with his family was atypical. Was his choice of occupation an attempt to escape the tension with his family?

5. The animosity of "enemies" of the Mormons toward Porter Rockwell and the Church in general is, perhaps, understandable. But how can you explain the hostility of formerly powerful Church members such as Sam Brannan, John C. Bennett, and Emma Smith Bidamon toward the Mormons in general and Rockwell in particular?

6. If Porter Rockwell did attempt to murder Lilburn Boggs, either at the behest of Mormon authorities or on his own, could such action be justified based on the treatment Mormons received in Missouri?

7. Lilburn Boggs not only survived the assassination attempt, he went on to a successful and influential "second life" in California. What does his continued prosperity say about the morality of or accountability related to his actions against the Mormons?

8. All contemporary accounts indicate that after coming West, Boggs and Rockwell lived with a certain amount of fear and uncertainty concerning the intentions of the other. Does this seem justified? Why or why not?

9. While a relatively minor character in the story, Calvin Pogue's daughter, Emily Elizabeth, is never far from his thoughts. How does his love for her affect his actions in the book, and how does it change him?

10. Do you think Porter Rockwell did it?

ABOUT THE
AUTHOR

A VERSATILE WRITER, Rod Miller is author of two nonfiction books, *Massacre at Bear River: First, Worst, Forgotten* and *John Muir: Magnificent Tramp*; a Western novel, *Gallows for a Gunman*, and two collections of poetry, *Things a Cowboy Sees and Other Poems* and *Newe Dreams: Poems by Rod Miller*. He has also written many essays, magazine articles, book reviews, and anthologized short stories, and his poems have appeared in numerous magazines and anthologies.

Born and raised in a small town in Utah among horses and cattle, and a veteran of the rodeo arena, he comes by his love of the West and its history, culture, and people honestly. He is a member of Western Writers of America.